BE MINE

Book 5 in the Fircrest Seriess

SHANNON GUYMON

Be Mine
Book 5 in the Fircrest Series
By Shannon Guymon

This book is dedicated to everyone who believes in happy endings!

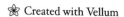 Created with Vellum

Chapter One

KISS AND TELL

Taryn's Birthday Party

Kam watched as Wren walked out of the restaurant with Rob and shook his head slightly.

"*Why the frown*? Aren't you glad to see them back together?"

Kam turned and looked down into the beautiful face of Bailey Downing, Rob's youngest sister. "I'm more worried right now. Looks like Rob has a second chance. I just hope he doesn't mess it up this time," he said, glancing back at the door.

Bailey frowned and crossed her arms over her metallic dress. "Okay, Rob has made some mistakes, but so has Wren. Have a little faith."

Kam grinned and turned his whole attention back to Bailey. "I have plenty of faith. What about you?"

Bailey's eyebrows went up and she smiled slightly. "I have plenty of faith in my brother. He's the best man I know," she said, with a proud tilt of her head.

Kam stepped closer and took her hand, pushing the large metal bracelets she was wearing, up her arm. "Nah, I'm talking faith in love. Do you have any?"

Bailey licked her lips and looked away from him, as he continued to play with her bracelets. "Sure, of course I do," she said breezily.

Kam watched the way her eyes narrowed and her mouth turned down. "Faith takes action, Bailey. You should go out with me."

Bailey's eyes turned wary as she smiled faintly. "I really wish I could, Kam, but my social calendar is kind of full at the moment," she said, and with a little wave, turned around on her high heels and began walking away.

Kam frowned darkly at her back and without thinking, he moved forward, grabbing her hand and pulling her down the hallway, and toward the empty kitchen.

"*Hey!* What are you doing?" Bailey squawked, pulling on her hand as he pushed open the door, and flipped on the light.

He let go and looked down at her with his hands on his hips. "So, what was this, Bailey? You spend all night flirting with me, and talking to me, and playing me up, and when I take the bait, you just swim away with a little wave of your hand. I didn't take you for shallow and cruel, but that's what it's starting to look like," he said grimly.

Bailey's mouth fell open and she shook her head. "Just because a girl talks to you, doesn't mean she wants to *date* you. I guess you're just used to all the girls falling at your feet, so it comes as a shock when I don't. Well, here's some advice, Kam. Grow up, buddy and get used to disappointment. Now, I'm bored, so just move out of my way," Bailey said, with a queenly flick of her wrist.

Kam's face cleared and he nodded his head. "Ah, I get it now. You were just using me. You were getting me out of the way, so Rob could make his move."

Bailey bit her lip and looked at her feet for a moment. "I don't use people," she said tightly, starting to look mad.

Kam leaned back against the door and crossed his massive arms over his chest. "Yes, Bailey, as a matter of fact, you do. You used my attraction for you against me, so you could get your way. Add manipulative to that list."

Bailey crossed her arms over her chest, mirroring Kam and tapped her foot on the floor angrily. "You're a jerk. Now, get out of my way," she hissed, and moved forward, assuming Kam would move as well.

Kam's eyes gleamed darkly at Bailey before he moved. He grasped Bailey's upper arms and pulled her up against his chest, before leaning down and kissing her. Bailey immediately stopped pulling away and began kissing him back. Kam lifted his head after a few moments and stared with hard eyes, down into Bailey's unfocused blue eyes.

"See you around, Bailey," he said, and turned and walked out of the kitchen, letting the door swing shut.

Bailey stood where she was, looking dazed and feeling a little wobbly. She lifted a hand to her lips and then closed her eyes briefly.

"*Wow.*"

Chapter Two

BAILEY'S BOYFRIEND

Two Months Later

Bailey breezed through the offices of the News Tribune, and waved at a few colleagues before plopping down on her old, blue rolling chair that always made her back ache. Today was a good day. Today she had a date with Dean Hogan. Dean was the perfect man for her. He was older, successful, intelligent, but yet fun and sweet too. *And now, he was hers.*

She twirled around on her chair one more time before opening her laptop and glancing over her emails. She felt her mind wandering and grabbed her cell phone where her home screen was dedicated to Dean's picture. Bailey smiled softly and sighed. Dean looked like a better looking Ben Stiller. Dark, thin and yet strong. But it was his smile that got to her every time. She closed her eyes and forced herself to put her phone away.

It would be their third date tonight and she was already feeling flutters in her stomach just thinking about it. They'd hugged and held hands, but he hadn't kissed her yet. *Yet.* Tonight that was going to change and she couldn't wait. It had been a long time since she'd allowed a man to get close enough for a kiss. She didn't count Kam Matafeo's kiss, because that had been just revenge.

Bailey shook her head to clear the memory of that one kiss and gritted her teeth. Kam Matafeo had a talent for getting her off track. He was always sneaking into her mind at the strangest times. *Dean.* That's who she was thinking about. Dean Hogan, her future boyfriend, if she had anything to say about it.

She hadn't dated anyone seriously in years and her mom, Anne Downing, had been on her back about it constantly. Fortunately for her, with Rob's wedding coming up, he'd taken the heat off of her and her sister, Taryn. *Thank you, Rob.* She kissed her fingers and touched her older brother's picture on her desk. He was the best brother any girl could ever ask for. Kind, generous and fun. Rob always had her back and she would always have his.

She couldn't wait for Rob to meet Dean. She had talked up her brother's restaurant so much, Dean had asked her if it was okay if they had dinner at The Iron Skillet tonight. Which reminded her, she needed to stop by the restaurant at lunch to warn her brother she was bringing Dean tonight. She wanted everything to be perfect. She would even request Wren, the head chef and future sister-in-law, to come out and talk to them.

Wren was so sweet and beautiful, she'd leave an impression for sure. And if Rob would come out and introduce himself, it would be perfect. Dean would look at her family and know how amazing they were. Taryn would be hanging around too, so he could practically meet the whole family all in one night.

Bailey glanced at her mother's picture sitting on her desk and winced. She'd wait to introduce Dean to her mom for as long as possible. She loved her mom, but she was a strong woman, who didn't believe in subtlety. She could picture it right now, Anne grilling Dean on why he hadn't proposed to her yet. She grinned thinking of Wren's first meeting with Anne and how her mother had accused her of being a teenager and had ordered her out of the church. Bailey snorted, as a giggle slipped out and grinned.

Nope, Dean would have to wait to meet Anne, which meant that she'd have to swear Taryn and Rob to secrecy about her social life. Because if her mom caught wind of any man on her horizon, she would be all over that and insist on having him over for a Sunday dinner. And that was not going to happen. Dean would run for the nearest exit and she wouldn't blame him.

Bailey worked all morning on an article she was writing about Common Core and the school district, before a meeting she had with the editors. After stopping by to speak to the principal of Wilson High School, she headed to The Iron Skillet. She parked her little, silver Hyundai and hurried inside. She waved at Brittany, the hostess and walked back to Rob's office. The door was always open, so she walked in and stopped in her tracks.

"*Yuck!*" she yelled, making her brother and Wren jump apart.

Rob glared at her and slipped his arm around Wren's shoulders. Wren grinned at Bailey and leaned up to kiss Rob on the cheek.

"Gotta get back to the kitchen. Come back and say hi when you're done with Rob, Bailey. I just made the most amazing dish. Truffle cream, Mac and Cheese. You'll die, it's so good."

Bailey licked her lips and closed her eyes as she imagined just how good that was going to taste. "You are the best future sister-in-law I've ever had, even if you are always kissing Rob."

Wren laughed and walked out, leaving her alone with her brother. Bailey, still grinning, turned back to Rob and blinked when she noticed he was still frowning at her.

"*What?* The door was wide open. Come on, you can't be mad at me. I'm impressionable. It's not right to walk in on a PG-13 situation, when I was expecting to find you sitting at your desk working."

Rob rolled his eyes and sat down with a sigh. "You're twenty-four not, thirteen and yelling, *Yuck,* every time you see my fiancée and I kissing is getting old. I'm starting to think you have some very serious hang ups," Rob said, looking at his sister with serious eyes.

Bailey blushed as she sat down across from her brother. "Well, since I'm positive you don't have a Ph.D. in psychology, I don't think we need to have that conversation, but to make you happy, I'll try to restrain myself in the future. *Okay?*"

Rob narrowed his eyes and shrugged. "Whatever, so what is so important that you had to interrupt Wren's break with me?"

Bailey frowned guiltily and bit her lip, starting to feel crappy about interrupting Rob and Wren. "I just wanted to let you know that I'm bringing someone special by for dinner tonight. Dean Hogan. I've gone out with him a couple times and tonight is our third date and I just want it to be really nice."

Rob's grumpy expression immediately cleared and he grabbed his cell phone sitting on the desk. Bailey gasped and dove for the phone, but Rob was faster and turned his chair around so she couldn't grab it away. Bailey groaned and ran around the desk, jumping on her brother's lap and covering the mouth piece, just as she heard her mother's voice come over.

"*Rob?* Is that you? . . . ."

Bailey snarled as Rob attempted to answer their mother. With her last ounce of strength, Bailey pulled the phone out of her brother's hand, sending her flying toward the carpeted floor, with an impact that left her breathless and bruised.

Rob loomed over her and she quickly disconnected the call.

"You're the most evil man in the world," Bailey gasped, as she sat up with a groan.

Rob grinned evilly and nipped his phone out of her hand. "Are you ever going to interrupt me or embarrass Wren *ever* again, when you catch us kissing?"

Bailey stood up and rubbed her behind with a scowl on her face. "No, I won't."

Rob glanced at the phone as it began to ring, and raised an eyebrow at his sister. "*Promise.*"

Bailey felt her heart pound in her chest as Rob held the phone next to his ear. "I promise!"

Rob smiled victoriously. "Hi, Mom, sorry we got disconnected. My phone's been acting up on me. I was just calling to tell you I love you and I'm so grateful that you're helping me and Wren with all of the wedding preparations."

Bailey watched him, as she held her breath, begging him silently, not to tell her to come to the restaurant for dinner that night.

"Oh, you're walking right now? Okay, we'll talk later. Bye, mom," he said, and disconnected.

"You don't know who you're messing with, Sis."

Bailey glared at Rob and stuck out her tongue. "You're the meanest, older brother anyone's ever had."

Rob laughed and pulled out his candy drawer, grabbing an *Almond Joy* and throwing it to her. "Not that mean. Irritated, *yes,* mean, *no.* As a matter of fact, I'll even be nice to your date tonight. I've heard of Dean Hogan. He's a successful psychologist from Tacoma, right? He's kind of a player, Bailey. What are you doing with him?"

Bailey opened the candy bar with a frown and crossed her legs. "He's dated a lot in the past, but that doesn't make him a player. Jeez, Rob, *you* dated everyone from Olympia to Canada, and you weren't a player."

Rob snorted and put his hands behind his head. "Just be careful. You're beautiful, smart and amazing, and I don't want to see you as just some guy's arm candy for the night."

Bailey sighed and threw her wrapper in the waste basket, making a perfect two points. "Rob, you're being cynical. I really like this guy. Our last two dates were incredible. I enjoy being with him. He's nice and sweet and interesting and he's been a perfect gentleman so far."

Rob shrugged and looked out the window. "We'll see. Bring him by tonight. I'll save you guys a good table and I'll stop by to say hi. We'll show him a good time, *but watch out.* Third dates are when men make their moves. Remember, you don't have to kiss him if you don't want to."

Bailey laughed and stood up. "I *want* to kiss him. As a matter of fact, I can't wait,"

"I'm right here. Proceed when ready."

Bailey whipped her head around to see Kam Matafeo, leaning in the doorway with an amused smile on his face.

Bailey felt her face redden as she grabbed her purse off the chair. "Eavesdropping, Kam? Kind of sad."

Kam grinned and walked into the room, taking up way too much space and making her feel small. "I just assume any time you're talking about kissing, you're talking about me. Well, here I am. Don't let me stop you," he said, bending down so they were face to face.

Bailey blinked in surprise as she stared at Kam's beautifully sculpted mouth and swallowed nervously. "I was talking about my date tonight, *not* you. See you around, Rob," she said, and hurried out of the office, wondering why in the world her heart was pounding so hard.

She hurried toward the kitchen and hoped Kam would take his time with Rob so she could taste the mac and cheese, without his overpowering presence in the kitchen. Luckily, Wren already had a small bowl waiting for her, so she kissed Wren on the cheek and hurried back out to go in search of Taryn. No surprise, she found her talking to a group of waiters and waitresses.

Bailey stood back, leaning against the bar as she watched her older sister in action. Taryn looked more like Rob, dark, dramatic and interesting looking. She had that amazing wavy, dark, brown hair and dark eyes. She grinned as she noted Brogan was standing next to Taryn. Brogan had had a crush on Taryn ever since his sister Kelly had brought Taryn home for a school project, they'd worked on together. As gorgeous and smart and funny as Brogan was, Taryn refused to take him seriously because he was three years younger than her. Bailey felt a little sad about that and decided to see what she could do to help her sister see past their age differences.

Taryn caught sight of her and smiled. Bailey lifted her spoon in a salute and waited a few more minutes until Taryn was done. Brogan walked over and gave her a one armed hug as he glanced down at her now empty bowl.

"Truffle cream Mac and Cheese? Good choice. Best thing I've ever tasted in my life," Brogan said, before wandering off.

Bailey grinned and waited as Taryn walked toward her, her eyes still on Brogan's disappearing back though. "Hey, Bailey, what are you eating?"

Bailey showed her the empty bowl and grimaced. "Wren insisted I taste the most delicious thing ever created, and now I need a second helping. Come sit with me while I order up more truffle cream, Mac and Cheese."

Taryn grinned as they walked toward their favorite booth. "Brogan couldn't shut up about it, and now my mouth is watering. I'll get some breadsticks to go with it."

Within minutes they had steaming bowls in front of them and with twin grins they dug in. Taryn's moans of pleasure made Bailey giggle as she glanced around the busy restaurant. Brogan lifted his head and winked at them, before turning back to his customer.

"Taryn, knock it off. People are staring."

Taryn opened her eyes and sighed happily. "Have I told you lately how much I love Wren? Do you realize that we're going to have a professional chef as a sister-in-law? Just think about Thanksgiving and Christmas."

Bailey smiled contentedly. "Yeah, Rob should be commended for bringing such talent to the family."

Taryn licked her lips and took a sip of water as she studied her younger sister. "So, why are you so happy? You look like you've been swimming in a pool of truffle cream Mac and Cheese."

Bailey laughed and picked up a fragrant, buttery breadstick as she sat back. "Taryn, you won't believe this, but I swear I have a boyfriend."

Taryn choked on her water and stared at her as she coughed. When she could speak, she shook her head. "I'm not falling for that again. You never date a guy more than once. April Fool's was last month."

Bailey frowned and put her breadstick down. "Just because I don't date very much doesn't mean I never date. And I'm not kidding. I'm bringing him here tonight for dinner, so I want you to come out and say hi to him and be charming and gracious."

Taryn's eyebrows shot up and she sat forward. "*You're serious.* You're really bringing a man here to the restaurant."

Bailey nodded her head and then sighed as Taryn reached for her cell phone. "Call her and you're dead."

Taryn frowned and put her cell phone back in her pocket. "Sorry, it's just I can imagine Mom's face right now. Joy and shock and wonder all at once. So, tell me about him. How did this guy win your heart, over all others?"

Bailey relaxed and took another bite before answering. "Taryn, it's hard to explain, but he's just perfect. Picture the perfect man for me and Dean is it. He's so smart and educated. He's older than me, so he's mature and solid too, which I love and he says the sweetest things to me. Taryn, I've never been treated so well in my life. He's charming. That's the word for him. Men just *aren't* these days. But he is. He thinks I'm beautiful," she said softly.

Taryn narrowed her eyes at Bailey and sat back, crossing her arms over her chest. "Sounds like a real smooth talker."

Bailey nodded her head immediately. "All men should take lessons from Dean on how to treat a woman. The world would be a much better place."

Taryn snorted, but smiled and waved her hand in the air. "I look forward to meeting him tonight. I've never seen you so loopy over a man before. If he can put a smile that big on your face, then I already like him."

Bailey sighed happily and nodded. "You'll see, Taryn, he's

perfect for me. I can't wait to change my Facebook status to, *in a relationship*. Maybe tonight he'll ask me to be his girlfriend."

Taryn bit her lip and frowned a little at her. "Bailey, you're kind of jumping in with both feet here. Sometimes it's good to be a little cautious this early in the game, just so you don't get your hopes up, because trust me, it hurts when reality doesn't match up to the fantasy we create in our hearts."

She blinked in surprise at her sister and sat up. "Taryn, come on. You're my big sister. Everyone's been waiting for me to take dating seriously and now that I am, you're sitting there and telling me to slow down? Well, I'm not going to. I'm going to enjoy every second of this relationship. I'm going to slurp up all the anticipation, the excitement and the romance. Taryn, I want the butterflies, and I can't have those without jumping in with both feet."

Taryn grinned and shook her head. "Fine, I'm with you then. I want you to have as many butterflies as your little tummy can handle. Now give me the rest of your mac and cheese."

Bailey laughed and pushed her bowl toward her sister. With her brother and sister in her corner, tonight was going to be a big success. She had a good feeling about her new boyfriend.

Chapter Three

PRINCE CHARMING

Bailey scanned the restaurant as she and Dean walked inside. Everything looked great. It was a Friday night, so it was packed and the smells coming from the kitchen were so good, her stomach jumped in excitement.

"Dean, you're going to love the food," she said, over her shoulder.

Dean's warm, brown eyes glowed down at her, as he put his hand on the small of her back. "I'm already sold. This place is amazing. I can't believe I've never eaten here before," he said, smiling as he glanced around.

Brittany winked at Bailey and escorted them back to one of the best tables. It was in the back, secluded from other tables, and had romantic candle light and fresh flowers waiting for them. Bailey grinned and made a note to get Rob a good birthday present.

After being seated and handed their menus, Brittany disappeared and Brogan took her place, filling their water glasses and making suggestions. Bailey was used to Brogan laughing and joking around with her and her friends, so Brogan being completely and flawlessly professional, was new to her. He grinned at her before walking away, and she smiled in appreciation.

Dean glanced up from the menu and smiled at her. "Bailey, I really owe you. I'm going to have to bring all my future dates here. The menu is first class, the service is incredible and the ambience is warm and inviting. If the food can match everything else, I'm going to be very impressed with your brother."

Bailey's eyes widened at the comment about bringing other women to the restaurant, but his twinkling brown eyes had her laughing. *What a joker.*

"Well, get ready to be impressed, because I know Wren Tyler, the head chef, and she's an artist with food. She's so creative and fun and exciting. It's like she puts her whole heart and soul into everything she prepares, and you can tell. Food created with love tastes better. You'll see, Dean. What are you going to order? I can vouch for the truffle cream, Mac and Cheese as an appetizer. I had some earlier and I'm obsessed now."

Dean shook his head. "Nah, that sounds kind of heavy. I think I'll go with the French onion soup, the salmon and the polenta. What are you having?"

Bailey bit her lip as she glanced at the choices. "I think I'll have the same. It's hard to go wrong here. There's nothing I don't like on the menu."

Brogan appeared immediately with the bread basket, took their order and disappeared. Bailey wondered why Dean wasn't looking at her, as they continued to talk and chat, but put it down to his curious nature. He was so intelligent and everywhere they went together, he just soaked up everything around him.

Dean glanced at her, blushing a little, before clearing his throat. "Sorry, Bailey, I know it's rude not to look at you when you're talking to me, but it's just so hard to look at you sometimes."

Bailey frowned and looked away. "What do you mean?" she asked quietly.

Dean reached over and grabbed her hand in his. "Your eyes

are so beautiful, it's hard to catch my breath. Sometimes I look at you, and I can't believe how lucky I am to be the man sitting with you."

Bailey raised her head and looked across the table at Dean and felt her heart melt as he stared at her, his brown eyes warm and sincere. "Dean, that is the sweetest thing anyone's ever said to me," she whispered.

Dean smiled and looked down at their entwined hands. "You know, I've been dating for so long, but I'm starting to think that what I want is commitment. I'm getting so tired of dating, aren't you?"

Bailey felt her heart speed up, as she realized Dean was leading somewhere very important. She'd heard of relationships getting serious after the third date, but she'd never believed it. *Now*, she believed it.

"I couldn't agree more," she said, glancing down at his mouth and wondering what it was going to be like to kiss him later that night.

Brogan appeared and refilled their water glasses so smoothly, Bailey vowed to help him out with Taryn. Rob showed up just as Brogan walked away with a plate of calamari in his hands.

"You two look like you could use an appetizer."

Bailey grinned happily and gestured to her brother. "Dean, I want to introduce you to my big brother Rob, the best brother in the whole world," she said, and then stood up to give Rob a quick hug.

Rob smiled at Bailey and kissed her on the cheek, before looking at Dean. Dean smiled politely and stood up, holding his hand out.

"Hi, Rob, it's nice to meet you. Bailey talks about you and Taryn all the time."

Rob smiled and grabbed a chair from the next table, pulling it over and sitting next to her. "That's Bailey, she's a sweetheart."

Bailey placed her napkin in her lap and picked up a piece of crispy calamari, dipping it in the spicy sauce, as her brother and Dean talked about the restaurant and Pacific cuisine.

"So, you two have been dating for a little while now, I take it?" Rob asked, putting his arm around the back of her chair.

Dean nodded his head and smiled at Bailey. "We've been out a couple times. I love going out with your sister. Anyone looking at Bailey on my arm, knows I'm a lucky man."

Rob narrowed his eyes at that, but Bailey smiled, feeling her heart swell. Dean was the best boyfriend in the world.

"So, are you guys exclusive then?" Rob asked with a polite smile.

Dean had been taking a sip of water and immediately started to choke. Rob stared grimly at Dean, as Bailey frowned and handed Dean a napkin.

Dean coughed into his napkin a few times, his eyes turning red before putting his napkin back on the table. "*Exclusive?* Are you asking if Bailey and I are in a committed, monogamous relationship?"

Rob nodded his head, not smiling anymore. Bailey frowned and elbowed Rob in the side. *What was he doing? Sabotaging her date?*

Dean glanced at her, looking uncomfortable all of a sudden, which made her feel uncomfortable too.

"This is our third date, Rob. I think it's fair to say that Bailey and I are still getting to know one another. But if that changes, you'll be the first to know," he said smoothly.

Rob gave Dean a half smile and stood up. "Well, I'll let you two get to know each other better then. Bailey, let me know if you need anything. Have a good evening," he said, and wandered off.

Bailey watched him go with a frown on her face. Rob had looked so suspicious and cold. *What was going on?*

"Wow, you've got a protective older brother, huh?"

Bailey looked back at Dean, smiling slightly. "Yeah, you could say that. Try this calamari, Dean. You'll think you're in heaven," she said, trying to get the date back on course.

Dean jumped at the chance to change the subject and soon they were laughing and relaxing again. Brogan brought their entrees and soon all talk turned to food.

"Bailey, this is the best meal I've had in months. Tell me more about your brother's chef," he said, taking another bite of the buttery polenta.

Bailey grinned and patted her mouth with her napkin. "She's a miracle. Rob just loves her. I asked her to come out tonight to meet you, so I hope she doesn't forget. I'll remind Brogan. She's kind of shy, but lately she's been coming out of her shell. She had a rough start here when she first started working for my brother. She was the sous chef and the head chef at the time, was completely horrid to her. We're lucky she didn't quit on us."

Dean nodded his head. "That would have been a tragedy. An accomplished and artistic chef is hard to come by. I should know. I think I've dated so much, that I've been to almost every single restaurant from here to Seattle," he said, laughing.

Bailey laughed too, but for some reason didn't find it all that funny thinking about all the women Dean had been out with. How was she going to compare to all of those women? She felt like shrinking, just thinking about it.

They talked and ate for a few more moments until Wren walked up to their table. Bailey grinned happily, noting Wren was wearing her chef's hat. Bailey thought it made her look like a chef from a fancy New York restaurant.

Wren put her hand on Bailey's shoulder. "Looks like you two are enjoying your meal. I'm surprised you didn't order more mac and cheese, Bailey," Wren teased.

Bailey laughed and gestured toward Dean, who was staring at Wren with an arrested expression on his face.

"Dean, this is Wren Tyler, the head chef of The Iron Skillet. Wren, this is . . . *um*, my friend, Dean Hogan."

Wren nodded her head to Dean and smiled warmly. "You are

one very lucky man to be here with Bailey. She's a beautiful, smart and interesting woman. You'll have to be on your toes to keep up with her."

Bailey blushed and squeezed Wren's hand. Future sister-in-laws were kind of nice. Especially Wren. Dean smiled and nodded, glancing at Bailey quickly.

"Bailey is an amazing woman, but I have to point out, that you yourself are pretty amazing too. You're one of the most talented chefs I've ever met. Your food is fresh and exciting and your talent is insane. I'm very impressed, Wren," he said, his voice warm and his eyes appreciative.

Bailey blinked in surprise. For a moment there, it almost looked as if Dean was flirting with Wren. She glanced quickly at Wren, but Wren was looking down at her feet of course. Sometimes she had a hard time talking to people she didn't know.

"Thank you, Dean. Well, I need to return to the kitchen, but I hope you enjoy the rest of your dinner. Be sure and try our Saffron Panna Cotta for dessert," she said, and with a quick smile at Bailey she walked away.

Dean watched her leave with a smile on his face, and shook his head moments later. "*Wow*, she's amazing isn't she?" he asked, picking up his fork again.

Bailey frowned. "Well, yeah. She is."

Dean took a bite of his salmon and closed his eyes in plea-sure. "Is she seeing anyone, do you know?" he asked innocently.

Bailey licked her lips and sat back in her chair, feeling cold all of a sudden. "I take it, you're interested in asking her out?"

Dean blinked and looked up at Bailey quickly. "Don't be silly, I was just wondering out loud if a woman that beautiful and talented, could be unattached."

Bailey nodded her head and pushed her fork through her polenta, making a figure 8 pattern. She opened her mouth to tell Dean, Wren was engaged to her brother, but Taryn took that moment to walk up to them.

Bailey smiled in relief, grateful her sister was there for some reason.

"So, this must be Dean. I saw your picture on Bailey's phone, but it does you no justice. You're way more handsome in person," she said, holding her hand out to Dean.

Dean grinned and stood up, shaking Taryn's hand firmly. "And who might you be?"

Bailey gestured toward Taryn with a proud smile. "Dean, this beautiful woman before you, is my older sister, Taryn. She's the manager here at The Iron Skillet, and my brother's right hand woman. She makes sure everything runs smoothly."

Taryn smiled at Bailey and grabbed the same chair Rob had taken earlier, sitting next to Bailey and motioning for Dean to take his seat. "That means you're dating the baby of the family, Dean. You up for that?" she asked, teasingly.

Bailey kicked Taryn's foot under the table, as Dean raised his eyebrow at her. "The baby of the family. You're not spoiled are you, Bailey?"

Bailey laughed and shook her head. "No, I'm the sane one of the family. Rob and Taryn got all of the wild Italian genes. I'm completely normal and very predictable."

Taryn snorted lightly at that, but smiled placidly. "Tell me about yourself, Dean. If I'm going to let you date my little sister, I want to know more about you."

Dean smiled charmingly and sat forward, looking earnest. "Well, as Bailey has told you, I'm a psychologist with a practice in Tacoma. My family is from Seattle and we've lived in the Pacific Northwest going back to the first settlers here. I have three younger sisters, so I know what it's like to feel protective of one. I don't have a police record and I have good credit. I hope I pass the test."

Taryn laughed and flicked her hair over her shoulder as Brogan appeared to refill their water glasses. "Can I bring you something to eat, Taryn?" Brogan asked considerately, his eyes twinkling down at her.

Taryn smiled and shook her head. "So tempting, but no. I won't hijack my sister's date. It was a pleasure meeting you, Dean. Come back anytime," she said, and stood up, putting her arm through Brogan's as she waved and walked away.

Dean laughed a little and looked around the restaurant. "Any other relatives lurking around you want me to meet?"

Bailey blushed, feeling embarrassed now, and wondering if Dean thought meeting her family was too soon in their relationship. "Well, this is a family run restaurant, but no. No one else tonight anyways. You still haven't met my mom. That will be interesting."

Dean frowned a little. "Meeting parents is kind of serious. Let's hold off on that."

Bailey frowned and nodded. "We can hold off as long as you want to on that," she said vehemently.

Chapter Four

BAD BOYS

Kam plated the pan seared halibut over a bed of faro, and looked up to see Wren frowning darkly as she stomped over to the sink to wash her hands. He could tell by the way she was muttering she was not happy.

"What's the matter, Little Bird? You look like you want to stomp on something," he said, with a grin. Wren didn't get mad too often, but when she did she simmered for a long time.

Wren gritted her teeth and took over the braised short ribs and pickled cabbage from Cynthia. "Thanks, I've got it now."

Kam raised an eyebrow, patiently waiting for Wren to tell him why she looked like a thunder cloud. Wren waited as Cynthia walked away, before turning back to Kam. She stood next to him, so no one else could hear.

"Kam, I hate Bailey's date. He's such a player. He was looking me up and down and flirting with me, right in front of her! I couldn't leave fast enough."

Kam frowned and handed the halibut off to a waitress. "Bailey's a big girl. She can handle men."

Wren shook her head, looking upset. "No, Kam, this guy is different. Whatever he's dishing out, Bailey is eating it up. I think she's really into this guy. I think she's going to get hurt."

Kam sighed and put his hands on his hips. "Wren, Bailey dates a different guy every week. And don't forget, I tried. She wasn't interested in me. Maybe she doesn't like good men. Maybe she's one of those girls, who likes the bad boys. Maybe she's addicted to drama and getting her heart broken. I think we should stay out of this."

Wren pouted and tightened her apron around her waist. "I think Bailey has everything twisted around. I think she looks at Dean and sees a good guy, and I think she looks at you and sees the bad boy. She just doesn't understand what she's doing."

Kam felt a headache brewing and massaged his head, as Brogan brought him a new order. "What do you think, Brogan? You like Bailey's boyfriend?"

Brogan snorted and massaged Wren's shoulders for a moment. "That guy is slick. But I hope Bailey doesn't fall for him."

Wren nodded her head in agreement, and took the order out of Kam's hand, moving to start the fried, soft shell crab that was a huge favorite with their customers. "Slick is the perfect word for Dean. Kam, go peek at him. See what you think."

Kam shrugged and glanced at the clock. He needed a break anyways. He'd grab a drink, take a peek at Bailey's man, and then go harass Rob for a minute. He took off his apron and sauntered out of the kitchen with Brogan at his side. Brogan pointed toward one of their best tables.

"Right there. Look at her face, Kam. She never looks at her other dates like that."

Kam scowled and glared at the man Bailey thought was the right one for her. More right than him, anyways. All he saw was a skinny, dark guy in a nice suit. He talked and laughed with Bailey, but his eyes were always scanning, as if he couldn't stop looking around.

Kam rolled his eyes and felt angry for some reason. "If that's the kind of guy Bailey wants, then she deserves him," he said, and turned and walked away.

He stomped down the hall to Rob's office and walked in without knocking. One of the waitresses was there, crying softly and Rob looked uncomfortable.

Kam put both of his hands up and tried to back out, but Rob saw him and shook his head. "Hey, Kam, I was wondering where you were. I thought you'd forgotten we had a meeting set up for now. Annette, I'm sorry things are so hard for you, right now, but I hope you don't quit on us. You're a fantastic waitress, and we'd be sorry to see you leave."

Annette, a darling little blond, nodded her head and gave a watery smile to Kam as she hurried out. Kam watched her leave with a pained smile, and took the chair she'd vacated.

"In love with Brogan?"

Rob sighed loud and long. "Does every waitress have to fall in love with that guy? I've lost more waitresses to broken hearts, than I can count."

Kam laughed and sat back, stretched out his back as he took a much needed break. "He needs to date one or two. If the girls knew he was in a relationship, they wouldn't fall so hard."

Rob rubbed a hand over his face and kicked his feet up on his desk. "He's focusing on his business, right now. That, and he's in love with Taryn. Oh, forget it. What can I do for you, Kam? You look mad. This isn't about the Rugby game tomorrow is it? You're coming right?"

Kam smiled and shook his head. "Of course, I wouldn't miss it. Nah, I just want to know what you think of Bailey's boyfriend. Wren went out to say hi, and he gave her an obvious once over and flirted with her right in front of Bailey. Brogan thinks he's slick, and I can't say I like the looks of him. What do you think?"

Rob frowned and grabbed a baseball off his desk and began throwing it up in the air and catching it. "I think she's going to get her heart broken, if she's not careful. And if that guy thinks he's getting anywhere near Wren, he's sadly mistaken."

Kam grinned. "You're such a jealous man, Rob. You've got to control all of those violent tendencies you have."

Rob laughed and threw the baseball to Kam who caught it easily. "Yeah, well tackling you and then having my ribs beaten in, cured me of a lot of my jealous tendencies. But there are a few still hanging around. Dean Hogan. Yeah, I'm going to have to say no to that guy. I'd hate to see Bailey's self-confidence take a hit, because her boyfriend can't stop flirting with every woman in a two mile radius."

Kam frowned and nodded. "Better get on it. She's falling for this guy."

Rob pointed a finger at Kam. "Can't you do something about this? Get in there and mess it up. Get Bailey's attention off this guy and where it belongs. *On you*. I keep telling you to ask her out."

Kam shrugged and threw the baseball up in the air a few times. "She's not ready for me. I scare her. All she sees when she looks at me, is a big Samoan guy with tattoos on his arm and no college degree. She wants some safe guy, in a suit and tie. I'm not who your sister wants. She wants someone like the guy she's with right now. He fits in with her image."

Rob glared at Kam and shook his head. "That's ridiculous. Bailey isn't shallow or for that matter, stupid. I don't care what you say. There's chemistry between you two. I've said it from the beginning. Bailey might not want to admit it, but she has a thing for you."

Kam threw the ball to Rob and stood up. "I'm not disagreeing with you. I know there's chemistry. I'm just saying she's making her choice. It's not me. It's that guy out there."

Rob stared as Kam walked away, frowning darkly. He stood up and grabbed his sport coat off the back of his chair and walked out onto the floor of the restaurant. He talked to a few diners as he kept his eye on his sister. He watched her body language and felt a moment of unease. And he also noted that Kam was right. Dean had a wandering eye. He shook hands with a regular customer, before making his way over to Bailey's table where they were sharing a dish of panna cotta.

"How was everything?" he asked, smiling brightly at his sister and her date.

Bailey beamed at him. "Rob, it was the best meal I've ever eaten here. Dean says he's going to come here from now on."

Rob smiled and looked at Dean, who was putting his napkin on the table. Dean smiled at Bailey and nodded his head. "She's right, Rob, it was perfect. I'd love to see your kitchen if you'd let us."

Rob remembered what Kam had said about Wren, and thought it would be the perfect opportunity to see Dean around his fiancee. If Kam was right, then he'd have the excuse he'd need, to talk to Bailey about dumping this guy.

"Absolutely. If you're done, you can follow me."

Bailey and Dean stood up and followed him back to the kitchen. He pushed through the door and smiled at the music playing in the background. Wren had Camila Cabello playing and everyone was singing along. Kam was already back to work and Wren was handing a plate off to Brogan. He watched Dean's expression as he saw Wren and went cold.

Dean was staring at Wren with a light in his eyes that he didn't like at all. Wren turned around and noticed them and her eyes lit up as they caught his. Rob restrained himself from going to her and pulling her into his arms for a kiss, like he usually did.

"I hope you don't mind the intrusion, but Bailey's date, Dean Hogan wanted to see our kitchen. Dean, what do you think?" he asked, gesturing to the clean and well-manned kitchen.

Dean put his hands in his pockets as he looked around with a smile on his face. "It's just how I pictured it. Wren, I have to tell you, I've never eaten anything as delicious as the salmon you made for me. I'm very impressed with you and I've eaten at the best restaurants in Seattle. I can't wait to come back and try all of your dishes."

Wren blushed a little and glanced at Rob quickly before answering. Rob smiled grimly at her and her smile faltered.

"Dean, you have a way with compliments. Thank you for

being so kind. I'm very glad you enjoyed my food. Bailey? Are you having a good time?"

Everyone turned and looked at Bailey, who was not smiling. She jumped a little and nodded her head, a big smile now replacing the frown. "Oh, yes. Dean is a wonderful date. The best. But we better let you get back to work though. Thanks for letting Dean see the kitchen."

Rob nodded his head and held the door open for Bailey and Dean to walk through. Instead of joining them, he walked over to Wren and pulled her into his arms, kissing her breathless before letting her go.

"What was that for?" she whispered, opening her eyes slowly.

Rob grinned and kissed her again. "Because I can. And because he can't. *Jerk.* What are you doing mesmerizing innocent diners, with your beauty and skill? I didn't realize how dangerous it was to let you out of the kitchen."

Wren laughed and pushed him in the chest. "You're hilarious. Now stop distracting me and go protect your sister from that guy."

Rob winced and nodded. "I can't do much protecting, if she won't let me. And I have a feeling that Bailey will have to figure this one out on her own."

Wren nodded sadly and leaned up and kissed him on the cheek. "I love you," she whispered, in his ear.

Rob grinned and hugged her tightly before walking out of the kitchen. He walked toward the front of the restaurant, calling out greetings to people as he watched Dean open the door for his sister.

As they drove away, Rob felt sad and helpless. Why did people have to get their hearts broken, before they learned who and what was good for them and who was bad for them?

Bailey woke up the next day, and stretched lazily. She smiled up at her ceiling and wondered if anyone had ever been as happy as she was. She rolled over onto her stomach and rested her chin on her hand, as she reached for her cell phone. She swiped the screen and Dean's face was immediately there, smiling back at her.

Last night had been wonderful. Amazing. *Perfect.* Dinner had been delicious and for some reason, eating while someone told you how beautiful you were, just seemed to make the food even better. The only downside to the night, had been when Dean couldn't seem to stop talking about Wren, but really, who wouldn't be impressed with her? She was an incredibly talented chef. Most people were in awe of that, so that was only normal. But he'd sure made up for it. The kiss at her front door, had been the best part of the entire night. He'd been sweet and tender and gentle with her. He hadn't made her nervous or uncomfortable at all.

Not like Kam.

Dean's kiss had been the complete opposite of Kam's kiss. Kam's kiss had been all heat and passion and Dean's kiss had been sweet and . . . *nice.* The kind of kiss that someone would give the girl, they're just about to ask for a commitment. Bailey frowned and flipped through her texts. Dean hadn't exactly asked her to be his girlfriend last night. She'd been kind of expecting him too, especially after he'd looked deep into her eyes and talked about how tired he was of dating and how he was ready to make a commitment. Kind of strange, but maybe he was the type of guy to take his time?

Bailey glanced at the clock and groaned. She'd promised Rob she'd come to his rugby game today. He was so used to his whole family going to all of his baseball games, he expected them to go to all of his rugby games too. He'd probably be eighty years old, playing chess and still insist that they show up to cheer him on.

Bailey grinned and hopped out of bed. She loved cheering on her brother. And he was just as good at showing up for everything to support her. She remembered the pageant her mother had forced her to enter, when she'd been sixteen. She'd won and Rob had cheered so loudly for her, he'd been asked to leave by the security. She laughed at the memory and hopped in the shower.

It was all about family with Rob. That's why she hoped Rob liked Dean. She couldn't imagine what she'd do if he didn't. But the way he'd been looking at Dean last night, made her nervous. He'd looked at Dean the way he'd look at someone from the opposite team, when he'd been playing professional baseball. He'd looked at him as if to say, *I honestly wouldn't mind hurting you.*

Bailey shivered under the hot stream of water and tried to think of something else. Taryn had seemed to like him. And she knew her mother would adore Dean. What woman could withstand those gorgeous brown eyes? No one she knew. Although she hoped *Wren* could.

Bailey winced and finished washing her hair. She hurried to comb it out and blow dried it quickly. She put on the bare minimum of makeup, grabbed some jeans and a t-shirt, an apple and a Life Water, and ran out the door. When she arrived at the playing field, she was only ten minutes late. Totally acceptable time frame.

She ran toward Wren and Jane and began yelling as loud as she could, so Rob knew she was there. She reached Wren's side, out of breath and grinning, as Jane laughed and shook her head at her.

"Okay, *okay*. He knows you're here. Now that we're all deaf," Jane said.

Bailey flipped her long, blond streaked hair over her shoulder and grinned. "Hey, I don't want to get in trouble for not being supportive. If I lose my voice, so be it. Did you bring any cupcakes, Jane?" she asked in a small, pleading voice that had Wren giggling.

Jane made a huffing sound, but pulled out a large bakery box and opened it for her. "Take your pick. Take two. You're too skinny."

Bailey stuck out her tongue and picked the large Matafeo cupcake. "Bless you, Jane. There has to be a special place in heaven for bakers. And chefs too," she said, glancing at Wren.

Wren laughed and whistled loudly for Rob, as he made a tackle. "Thanks, Bailey. Jane, where was it journalists went after death? I can't remember. Was it heaven?"

Jane raised an eyebrow teasingly and glanced at Bailey. "I thought we agreed not to tell Bailey about hell, until she was older?"

Bailey laughed at that and bumped her hip into both of theirs. "And to think I've written such beautiful reviews of Belinda's Bakery and Wren's cooking. Such a shame. I guess I'll have to give into my evil nature, and rip you guys apart next time."

Wren laughed and put her arm through Bailey's as the opposite team cheered after scoring. "Oh, crud. Rob's going to hate that," she muttered.

Bailey winced and took another bite as she actually started to pay attention to the game. Taryn showed up ten minutes later, with her hair in a ratty ponytail and looking bleary eyed and half

dead. She would definitely win the best sister award that day.
She'd been almost on time and she yelled louder.

"What happened to you? You look like you had a hot date
last night. That, or you just didn't go to sleep," she said, looking
Taryn up and down critically.

Taryn turned red and ran a hand over her wild pony tail.
"None of your business, Bailey. Jane, I'll give you twenty dollars
for a cupcake."

Jane silently opened the box and offered it to Taryn. She
picked the second largest Matafeo cupcake, and bit into it with a
loud groan of appreciation. "You just saved my life," she
murmured, her whole face now covered in chocolate.

Bailey shook her head and handed her a napkin. "Girl, pull it
together. You look like a homeless zombie."

Taryn glared at her while Jane and Wren laughed.

"*Speaking of hot dates.* How was last night, Bailey? Did Dean
ask you to be his girlfriend?" Jane asked, her eyes wide and
curious.

Wren frowned and looked at her quickly. Bailey licked her
lips and shrugged, feeling kind of stupid now for telling everyone
that Dean was her boyfriend. If he *felt* like a boyfriend, didn't
that make him her boyfriend? She glanced at Wren's worried
expression, Taryn's curious eyes and Jane's gleeful expression and
sighed.

"Not exactly, but it *was* the best date ever. And the kiss was
sweet," she said, with a grin.

She heard a whistle and the team rushed over to the side to
grab water bottles, ending their conversation. She had to admit
she was grateful for some reason.

"Hey, Bailey, thanks for showing up for me," Rob said, kissing
her on the cheek and glaring at Taryn.

Taryn's mouth fell open and she put her hand on her waist.
"Just be grateful I showed up at all, Rob. I'm exhausted. You
know how busy Friday nights are. And then to have to be to a
game at nine, the next morning? You should be shot."

Rob laughed and kissed Taryn on the cheek too, making her glare and push him away. "Ick! You're sweaty."

Rob took the water bottle Wren held out to him. "I'm glad you're here, Sis," he said, as he wrapped his arms around Wren.

Bailey smiled at her brother and Wren. On the outside they didn't look like a good match, but for some reason they were like two puzzle pieces that completed each other. It worked. And Wren didn't seem to mind how dirty and sweaty her brother was.

"Thanks for coming to cheer for me, Bailey. I love hearing you scream my name," Kam said, behind her.

Bailey slowly turned to face Kam and lifted an eyebrow. "Is *your* name Rob?"

Kam grinned and took a drink out of his water bottle, his long wavy black hair pulled back in a ponytail. "Were you yelling for Rob? I could have sworn you came to cheer for me. I'm your favorite player, aren't I?"

Bailey laughed and shook her head. Kam always made her laugh with his outrageous flirting. "You're my favorite cupcake, that's for sure. Those Matafeo cupcakes are right up there with Wren's truffle cream Mac and Cheese."

Kam glanced at the cupcake in her hand and raised an eyebrow. "Give me a bite, I can't remember what they taste like."

Bailey glanced around the people surrounding them, but Wren and Rob were talking to Taryn, and Jane had run off to be with Tate, leaving her and Kam on their own. She bit her lip and shrugged. *Why not?* She could be nice and share. She lifted the cupcake to Kam's mouth and he grasped her hand lightly in his, guiding the cupcake. He took a large bite of the cupcake, staring into her eyes the entire time. Bailey swallowed and felt warm all of a sudden. Kam chewed his bite, keeping his hand on hers.

"You're right, they're delicious," he finally said. "But I'm still the best Matafeo there is," he said, stepping closer to her.

Bailey stared up into Kam's strong, handsome face and felt her stomach drop suddenly. She stepped back when loud laughter pierced the fog that had begun to surround her.

"*You're* the best Matafeo? Kam, come on. You're delusional. I believe *I'm* the only Matafeo out there today who's scored."

Bailey laughed and turned to see Jane and Tate standing next to them, grinning at Kam. Kam shook his head and crossed his massive arms over his chest.

"And you scored because of *my* tackle, that protected you. I believe I get half the credit."

Jane and Bailey exchanged laughing glances as Tate and Kam argued good naturedly. Jane grabbed Bailey's arm and pulled her to the side, away from the players.

"What's going on between you and Kam?" Jane asked curiously, glancing over Bailey's shoulder at the man in question.

Bailey glanced back at Kam, blushing at the insinuation. Right then, Kam glanced away from Tate and caught her eyes, sending a surprise bolt of electricity through her body. She blushed and looked away.

"*Nothing*, Jane. Are you kidding me? I'm dating Dean now. We're just friends," she said quickly.

Jane frowned at her and shook her head. "*Uh, uh*. Bailey, if there's one thing I know, it's Matafeo's and Kam Matafeo just ate a cupcake out of your hand, and then looked like he was going to snatch you up and start nibbling on you. And you, my friend, looked very willing."

Bailey's mouth dropped open and she began to sputter, as she felt a very large presence come to stand next to her. She closed her mouth and swallowed hard, looking up into the curious eyes of Kam and Tate.

"What are you two talking about, *hmmm*? You look very suspicious," Tate said, looking back and forth between the two women.

Bailey's eyes went wide as she stared at Jane. Jane grinned and put her arm around Bailey's shoulders. "Absolutely nothing, Tate. Nothing. At. All. Good luck out there," she added, as the whistle sounded.

Kam stared down at Bailey silently for a moment. "Well,

whatever you two were talking about, I'm going to find out. I have a feeling it was about me," he said, his eyes dark and serious.

Bailey watched as Kam and Tate ran back to the field and let a shaky breath out. "I don't know what it is about Kam, but I can never breathe right when he's around," she said softly, staring at him.

Jane laughed and let her arm drop off her shoulders. "That's exactly how I felt about Tate. I still can't breathe right when he's near me. But, here's the secret, Bailey. That's a *good* thing. A man that can steal your breath away, is very capable of stealing your heart."

Bailey frowned and forced herself to look away from Kam. "Well, that's where I disagree with you. I like Dean, because I can be perfectly comfortable around him. I've never once had trouble breathing around him."

Jane looked at her doubtfully, and shoved her hands in her jean pockets. "Wait, are you telling me you'd rather be around someone comfortable, than around someone exciting? You can't be serious, Bailey."

Bailey blushed and looked away. "Love doesn't need to be a roller coaster. I don't *want* the roller coaster. I know a lot of girls do, and that's fine for them. But for me, I've always wanted someone safe. Someone who is warm and kind and good. Someone I can depend on, you know."

Jane stared at her silently for a moment, and then reached out and touched her arm. "You've been hurt before, haven't you? Badly too."

Bailey closed her eyes for a moment as dark memories flooded in, uninvited. She pushed them back down and clenched her hands. "Maybe I have, so I think it's understandable to want someone like Dean, over someone like Kam. I don't think I could survive a relationship with Kam. Someone like him could take my heart, and I'd have nothing left when it was over."

Jane's brown eyes turned soft and sad, as she put her arm

around Bailey's shoulder again. "Honey, just because you and Kam have a lot of chemistry, doesn't mean he's not good and dependable and honorable. He's all of those things and more. It just feels dangerous to you, because what you're feeling is exciting. But Kam's not dangerous. Kam is a good, good man. He would never hurt you."

Bailey shook her head and closed her eyes. "I don't want to talk about it, Jane. Kam is a non-issue. Dean is the man I choose. Not Kam. Kam and I would never work. We're too different. Look at us. Could you really see Kam Matafeo and me as a couple?"

Jane glanced at Kam on the field and then back to her with a small sad smile. "Not only can I see it, I think it would be a wonderful thing for the both of you. Just don't rush things with Dean. Not yet."

Bailey tried to smile and pretended to be watching the game. "Jane, Dean is going to be my boyfriend. Forget Kam and me ever being together. It's never going to happen."

Jane grimaced and patted her back. "Okay, Bailey, if you say so. I need to go say hi to my sister, Layla. She just got here with Michael and the kids."

Bailey watched Jane run off to greet her sister and sighed miserably. Some people just didn't have a clue when it came to people, and Jane was one of them. Honestly, picturing her and Kam together as a couple. *What a joke.* Her eyes immediately found Kam on the field and she felt that familiar zip of adrenaline she got, every time she saw him. *Dangerous.* Kam Matafeo was a dangerous man and she couldn't gamble her heart on a man with long black hair and a large tribal tattoo on his arm. She could just imagine her mom's reaction if she brought Kam home for Sunday dinner. She laughed softly at the picture in her mind, and wished that she could have brought Kam home, just for her mom's reaction alone. It might be worth it.

Chapter Six

SUNDAY DINNER

Sunday afternoon Bailey, Taryn, Rob and Wren sat around the large wooden table, as Anne said the prayer over the food.

"And please bless Rob, for being such a good son. He's brought me so much happiness by getting engaged. We pray that Rob and Wren's love for each other will grow and multiply every day they're together. And please forgive Taryn and Bailey for breaking my heart. Neither one of my daughters has made any effort to find love. Please Father in Heaven, please grant unto me patience, as I try and be the best mother I can be. And I pray that my children will remember all of my sacrifices for their happiness. I pray that they will remember one of thy greatest commandments, to honor their mother..."

Bailey's mouth fell open as her mother closed her prayer, and she looked up to catch Taryn's eyes. Rob's snort of laughter and Wren's giggles just made her more furious. Taryn looked grim and ready to explode.

"Prayer shaming us, Mom? That's a new low," Taryn said tightly, grabbing the salad bowl and throwing a pile of lettuce on her plate, with so much anger it spilled over onto the table.

Anne sniffed and reached for the bowl of shrimp linguini. "If I have to call upon the powers of heaven, to help my family, then

I will. You can't blame me, Taryn. Rob's engaged and you haven't even been on a date. I'm horribly disappointed in you."

Bailey groaned and lowered her head into her hands. *Why, why did she come to these family dinners every Sunday?*

"And you, Bailey, floating through your life, completely unattached and happy to remain so. Well, I've had enough, do you hear me. I've had enough. You will take your love life serious, starting now, or I'll never forgive you," Anne said, throwing a pile of salad on her plate just as passionately as Taryn had done.

Bailey lifted her eyes and stared at Rob pleadingly. Rob's laughter died down as he saw that his two sisters were genuinely upset. Wren nudged him with her shoulder and he sighed loudly.

"Mom, we've talked about this before. You have to stop pressuring us when it comes to our love lives. Luckily for me, things worked out between me and Wren, and we fell in love, but you can't just point your finger and order people to jump into a relationship. It's not fair, it's not nice and I want you to stop. You're stressing out Taryn and Bailey, and they're doing the best they can. It's rough out there."

Anne's face turned red, and all of her anger turned on Rob. Rob gave her and Taryn a pointed look and she remembered why she loved Rob so much. He really was the best brother in the world. To distract their mom and point her anger away from her and Taryn, was probably the nicest thing anyone could ever do.

"I don't point my finger and order! Who do you think you're talking to, young man? I'm your mother. Everything I do, I do out of love. Do you think I like lecturing these girls about their responsibilities to this family? *Of course not.* I'd much rather be relaxing and enjoying a nice family meal together. But it's my duty as head of this family, since your father is gone, to make sure this family has a future. And that future is grandchildren."

Taryn moaned and hung her head dejectedly. Wren cleared her throat and raised her hand timidly. "Anne, if I may intrude, I'd like to point something out. Bailey *is* trying very hard to be a good daughter. She's been dating Dean Hogan for a while now, and although I think she could do better, I know she's trying. You have to give her credit for that at least."

Bailey's mouth fell open in horror. She slowly lifted her face and stared at the traitor sitting next to her brother. Wren smiled at her and winked. She shook her head as her mother's loud gasp of joy filled the dining room. She looked at her brother, and Rob winced, shaking his head apologetically. Taryn lifted her head and grinned at Wren, blowing her kisses before grabbing the bowl of linguine and dishing up a large serving, as all attention was now off of her.

"Wren, et tu Brute," she whispered, with a slow shake of her head, as Anne's squawks started to grow louder and louder.

Wren's face paled and she covered her mouth with her hand, as she realized she'd just done something very, *very* wrong. "Oh, Bailey, I'm so sorry," she whispered, in horror as she looked at Rob. Rob kissed her on the cheek and whispered in her ear, as Anne stood up and ran around the table to throw her arms around Bailey, hugging her so tightly, that her air supply was drastically compromised.

"Mom," she whispered, pulling on the surprisingly strong and wiry arms. "Mom, you're choking me," she tried again.

Anne immediately let go, leaning down to kiss her on the cheek. "Bailey, you are the best daughter in the world. Taryn should follow your example," she said, glaring at Taryn before sitting down.

"Now, tell me everything about Dean. What's he like? What does he do for a living? Do you love him?" she fired off, her eyes glowing with the light of victory.

Bailey sighed and pushed her plate away, not feeling hungry any longer. As she opened her mouth to respond, Rob jumped in.

"Mom, it was just a couple dates. They're not serious or anything. There's really nothing to report, right Bailey?" Rob said, with an encouraging smile at her.

Bailey smiled weakly, as her mother looked at her questioningly. She appreciated Rob's efforts to save her, but she didn't feel like lying to her mother. She was twenty-four years old, not fourteen. If she had a boyfriend, she wasn't going to lie about it.

"Thanks, Rob, but it's time mom found out. *Yes*, I have a boyfriend. His name is Dean and he's the most amazing man in the world. He has gorgeous brown hair, he's brilliant, he's sweet and he thinks I'm the most beautiful woman in the world."

Anne's face lit up brighter than a Christmas tree in March, as she clapped her hands. "Baby, I knew you had it in you. For years, I wondered if you hated men. I told your aunt Barbara just last month, you'd probably be single the rest of your life, but look at you! Going out on your own and finding a good man. Bless you, Baby. Now let's eat. I'm famished."

Bailey frowned at her mother, as Rob sighed loudly and Wren bit her lip nervously. Taryn grinned happily and took a sip of water. "We should invite him over for Sunday dinner next week, Mom. You could make your famous Lemon squares."

Bailey's eyes narrowed at her older sister, and she shook her head at the betrayal. "You evil, little witch," she breathed out, while Taryn just laughed.

Anne nodded her head and pointed to Wren. "Wren, sweetie, could you help me cook next week? I love those little crab cakes you make down at the restaurant. They're so light and full of flavor. And could you make some clam chowder to go with it too? Oh, and I love your panna cotta. I would be so grateful if you helped me out just a little."

Taryn giggled and Bailey even cracked a smile, as Wren turned to stare at Rob. Rob cleared his throat and leaned toward his mother. "Mom, Sunday is Wren's day off and you just basically asked her to cook the entire meal for us, next Sunday. I'm sure Wren could bring a dish, but she's not making the whole meal."

Anne made a huffing sound and patted her hard, shell like hair. "Well, you make it sound so horrible. I wasn't trying to overwork Wren, but you know how stressed out I get when you bring home the people you love. When you brought Wren home for the first time, I about had a heart attack I was so nervous. You don't want me to have a stroke or something do you?" she asked, in a small, sad voice.

Wren cleared her throat and looked at her hands, as she kicked Rob in the shins. Rob winced and nodded his head. "We'll bring the crab cakes. Taryn can grab a cake from Belinda's Bakery and Bailey can bring the salad. All you'll have to do, is make the clam chowder and that's easy. No stress."

Anne sniffed and put her nose in the air. "Well, if you think it's worth risking my health, then fine. I'll make the clam chowder. Bailey, have Dean here at one o'clock sharp. I can't wait to meet the man who was finally able to win your heart. He must be gorgeous," she said, relaxing and smiling as she chatted away merrily.

Bailey took a few bites of dinner and then escaped, leaving Rob and Taryn to help clean up the kitchen. She drove home, feeling a wall of gray slam down on top of her. Was Dean ready to meet her mother? Just Friday night, he'd acted very un-excited about the prospect, but they'd had such a great date, he might have changed his mind. He thought she was beautiful. He had told her flat out, he was sick of dating and wanted to commit. *It would be fine.*

When she got home, she texted Dean and asked him to lunch Monday. She'd take him to Belinda's for a croissant sandwich and a cupcake. He'd be putty in her hands. She smiled, feeling better about the situation. It would be fine. Dean would charm her mother, and he'd fall even more in love with her than he already was. Because he'd see how sane she was compared to how insane she could have turned out to be.

Chapter Seven

DEAN'S GAME PLAN

Bailey glanced at her phone screen for the tenth time and wondered why Dean was so late. He'd never been late before. He'd been so punctual, she could plan on him showing up right on the dot, every time. But now he was almost fifteen minutes late. She glanced back through her texts to make sure he'd actually agreed to meet her. She hoped he wasn't in a car accident.

Bailey bit her lip and stared out the window, as the soothing smell of chocolate surrounded her. If she was going to be stood up, Belinda's Bakery was the place to be.

"Late, huh?"

Bailey turned around in her seat and smiled at Kit Hunter, Jane's older sister. She didn't work very much at the bakery, but she came in when Jane needed a break or Layla had an appointment, or they just needed some time away. Kit was a professional artist, but she still loved making bread and hanging out with her sisters.

"He's fifteen minutes late, and he's never been late before."

Kit walked around the counter and sat down with her, pushing a chocolate dipped strawberry on a plate toward her. "On the house. If he's twenty minutes late, I'll let you try Jane's Crème Brule."

Bailey grinned and took a big bite of the juicy strawberry. "Okay, now I hope he's late."

Kit laughed and crossed her legs, swinging her long red hair over her shoulders. Bailey smiled over at her and noticed Kit's hand laying protectively over her stomach and her eyes widened. *No.* Kit, pregnant? She looked up at Kit's face and noticed her eyes were soft.

"Kit, are you expecting a baby?" Bailey whispered, sitting up and forgetting all about her date.

Kit grinned and nodded her head. "I'm almost three months now. My stomach is so pokey, I can't believe more people haven't noticed."

Bailey clapped her hands and ran around the table to hug Kit. "I'm so happy for you," she breathed out, still surprised. "You haven't been married that long either. Are you excited or nervous?"

Kit took a sip from her water bottle. "I'm sort of a mixture of every emotion that multiplied together equals something really close to complete joy. Bailey, there's nothing like loving a man with your whole soul, and then creating another little person because of that love. It's the most beautiful, incredible thing that's ever happened to me," she said, looking down at her stomach with wonder.

"I heard the baby's heartbeat this week and couldn't stop crying. And then Hunter started to cry, and we just held each other, right there in the doctor's office because we were now a family. Sorry, I'm rambling on and on, but I'm so happy, I have to share it with everyone or else I'll burst, " she said, with an embarrassed laugh.

Bailey shook her head and reached across the table to grasp Kit's hand. "No, don't be sorry. It's beautiful. What's happening to you and Hunter is the most beautiful thing that could happen between two people. Oh, wow, I want that," she whispered, closing her eyes.

Kit squeezed her hand as the bell sounded over the door.

The two women looked around and Bailey smiled as Dean walked in, looking embarrassed and just a little harassed.

Kit stood up and hugged her, before walking back around the counter. Bailey walked over to Dean's side and took his hand in hers. "I was starting to worry," she said, leaning up on her tiptoes to kiss him on the cheek.

Dean grimaced and kissed her lightly on the lips. "I'm sorry, Bailey. Hold up at the office. Forgive me?"

Bailey grinned and pulled him toward the display cases. "You're already forgiven. Now, you're going to love this, Dean. Belinda's Bakery has the most divine croissant sandwiches. And this is my treat, so I insist you have a cupcake for dessert. It won't be a perfect lunch without a cupcake."

Dean laughed and pointed to the turkey and pesto sandwich. "That looks incredible. I'll have that one and the red velvet cupcake with cheesecake filling."

Bailey smiled at his choice. "That sounds good, but I think I'll have a Reuben croissant and the Matafeo cupcake. I'll let you taste mine. It's so good, no other cupcake will ever do for me now."

Dean put his arm around her, as Kit got their lunches for them. Bailey noticed Dean smiled at Kit appreciatively, and then glance down at the ring on her finger. Bailey frowned and looked away. It was only natural of course. Kit was one of the most beautiful women in the world. Dean would have to be blind not to notice. She tried to push the negative thoughts away, but some of the joy of the afternoon faded.

Bailey took her tray and headed over to the farthest table by the window, so they could have some privacy. Dean joined her and immediately began eating. Bailey frowned, wondering if he was trying to eat quickly so their date could be finished. He hadn't even asked her out for Friday or Saturday yet.

"So, busy day, huh?" she asked, trying to start a conversation.

Dean looked up in surprise, almost as if he'd forgotten she

was there. "Oh, yeah, work is crazy. What about you? How did your um article on . . . the schools was it, go?"

Bailey frowned, wondering if he'd ignored her, when she'd been talking to him about her article on the Common Core. *Wow.*

"Yeah, life is busy when you're a reporter. Listen, I was wondering what you were doing this Sunday? My mom is having a big family dinner and your name came up yesterday, and she wanted me to invite you. What do you think?" she asked cautiously, looking at him.

Dean wiped his mouth and took a sip of his drink, before slowly lifting his eyes to hers. "Bailey, I thought we already discussed this and decided that you and I meeting each other's parents, wasn't something we would do."

Bailey felt her heart catch painfully, as she looked down at her half eaten sandwich in embarrassment. "Oh, well, it was just a thought. I mean, after our date on Friday and how well it went, I thought maybe you might want to change your mind. I mean, I really like you, Dean. And I thought that um, you really liked me too. What's the harm in taking things a step forward, if we know we're with the right person?"

Dean's face paled as he blinked at her. "Bailey, *wow*, I don't even know what to say. Look, usually I explain things to the women I date, but I thought you and I were kind of on the same page here. Um, when I told you I wanted to make a commitment and wanted to settle down and stop dating, what that meant was, that I'm going to spend this year dating as many women as I can. At the end of the year, I'm going to pick the woman who is the most compatible with me and my lifestyle. I like you too, Bailey, but I'm not just dating *you*. I'm sorry, I thought you knew that," he said, looking slightly disappointed in her as if she'd just failed his test.

Bailey felt as if she'd been hit by a truck she was so shocked. "You have to be kidding me," she whispered, looking away from

Dean's earnest face, and out the window at the misty Washington afternoon.

Dean reached over and grabbed her hand. "I really like you too, Bailey. I love being with you. You're beautiful, sweet and intelligent. You're practically perfect really, but I'd be doing myself a disservice if I quit looking now. I owe it to myself, my family, and of course my future children, to make sure I pick the best woman to be my partner. You understand don't you?"

Bailey nodded her head numbly. "Oh, yes, of course I understand. It's almost like your own little Bachelor show, huh?"

Dean frowned, looking confused. "The Bachelor show? What's that?"

Bailey laughed bitterly and shrugged. "Nothing. Listen, forget I invited you over for dinner on Sunday. It's no big deal. So, tell me, what hot date do you have lined up for this Friday and Saturday?" she asked, pasting on a cheerful smile, and picking up her sandwich and taking a big bite.

Dean grinned, relaxing again. "Well, I don't have a date lined up for this Friday *yet*, but I'm hoping to ask out your brother's chef. I was really impressed with Wren. I can't imagine what it would be like to date a professional chef. Can you imagine coming home from work, to a beautiful meal every night?"

Bailey nodded her head silently, as she fought the tears pounding to get out. She bit her lip hard and took a sip of cold ice water, hoping she wouldn't humiliate herself any more in front of this man. "And where do I fit in with your dating schedule?" she asked quietly.

Dean shrugged and took another bite of his sandwich. "Oh, don't worry, you're one of the top contenders. You're young, so that's a plus, you're gorgeous and educated and you have an interesting job. You're in my top ten for sure, so we can date a couple times a month, unless I get busy."

Bailey nibbled on the edge of her sandwich and wished she was far, far away on a deserted island. "Am I just supposed to wait around by the phone for you to call me then? Sorry, I guess I just don't understand how this works."

Dean laughed and sat back, patting his stomach happily. "Of course not, what kind of man do you think I am? Bailey, don't be silly, I'm a man who respects women. You're welcome to be out there dating too. Although when I call, I hope you make time for me, considering all the time I've spent on you. Listen, I'm going to take my cupcake to go, but let's stay in touch. This week is out of course, but next week, let's grab some dinner at your brother's restaurant. I don't think I'll rest until I've tried everything on the menu."

Bailey smiled up at Dean as he stood up and grabbed his cupcake. "And you'll get to see Wren at the same time, so it's almost like a bonus date, huh?"

Dean laughed and nodded his head, leaning down to kiss her on the cheek. "See, now you're thinking like me. Talk to you soon, beautiful," he said, with a wink and hurried out the door.

Bailey watched him go and felt like throwing up. *She had told everyone he was her boyfriend.* She'd put his picture on her phone. She'd told her mother he was coming for dinner. She should crawl off into the nearest dark corner and just die. Bailey lowered her head and groaned, as the reality of her situation crashed down upon her so hard, she felt bruises on her back.

"I take it things didn't go well?"

Bailey slowly lifted her head, her eyes filled with dark misery, and something close to shame. "No, not well," she said quietly.

Kit sat down and leaned forward, just as the bell rang over the door. "Oh, darn. Listen, stick around. I need to help this customer, but we need to talk. *Don't. Move.*"

Bailey lowered her head again, not caring if she ever moved again. If she didn't leave the bakery, then she would never have to tell Taryn or Rob *or her mom.* She groaned even louder at that thought and clenched her hands in her hair. The utter humiliation of falling for a player, even after her brother had warned her, felt like black, heavy tar surrounding her. Nothing could be worse than this. Nothing.

Ten minutes later, Kit rejoined her and nudged her shoulder gently. "Hey, you still alive?"

Bailey lifted her head again and shook her head. "Unfortunately."

Kit frowned and shook her head. "Hey, now, life is precious. Now, tell me what just happened or I'm going to call Taryn."

Bailey's mouth fell open in horror, and she grabbed Kit's hand. "Please, no. *Please*, I'm begging you don't call Taryn or Rob or anyone. As a matter of fact, I'll pay you to keep silent about this. Don't tell a single soul. Please, Kit," she begged.

Kit's eyes widened in surprise. "Bailey, I don't even know what happened! All I know is this guy waltzes in here twenty minutes late, and leaves ten minutes later, and you're a pile of misery. Whatever this is, it isn't good, and you need friends and support. Now, if I can't call Rob or Taryn, who can I call?"

Bailey felt a tear slip down her cheek and bit her lip to keep it from quivering, as she shrugged. "Jane. You could call Jane," she whispered.

Kit nodded her head and pulled out her cell phone, texting furiously as she glanced up at Bailey every now and then. "Done. Now if you don't want to tell me, you don't have to, but I'm a pretty good listener."

Bailey sighed and wiped her wet eyes with her napkin. "I was so dumb, Kit. So dumb. I took one look at Dean and built this beautiful fantasy in my head, you know. I thought he was the one for me. He made me feel beautiful and I could relax around him and we had fun. We'd been going out for just a little while, but in my head he was already my boyfriend. It was so real."

Kit frowned and nodded. "Well, sometimes relationships do happen that fast. Hunter and I did. So what happened?"

Bailey dipped her finger into the generous icing on her cupcake and licked her finger. "I asked him to go to dinner at my mom's house this Sunday, and he freaked out. He informed me that he was going to date as many women as possible in the next year, and then at the end of the year, he was going to pick the very best one. I have a good chance actually. He says I'm in the top ten so far."

Kit's mouth fell open and eyebrows jumped up. "You. Are. *Kidding*. Me."

Bailey shook her head slowly. "Would I make that up?"

Kit grimaced and ran her hands through her long red hair. "I hate men."

Bailey snorted at that and glanced at her stomach. "Yeah, I can tell."

Kit laughed and stood up as someone walked through the door. "Not all men, just the rotten ones. Oh, Bailey, you can do so much better than that. You're an incredible woman and if Dean didn't jump at the chance to be with you, and realize how grateful he should have been to even be with you, then it's his loss and I curse him to never find the right woman."

The older lady with a poofy gray perm, looked shocked at Kit's words and Bailey giggled. "Thanks, Kit. If you were a witch, I might really get a kick out of that."

Kit grinned over her shoulder. "Just ask your brother. He'll swear I'm the real deal."

Bailey gave up and laughed at that, and decided to finish her lunch. She'd paid for it after all, and she was going to need her energy to get through this new and horrible humiliation.

Five minutes later, Jane breezed through the door with a store bag on her arm from the mall. She caught sight of Bailey and hurried over, throwing her bag on the floor and pulling out a chair. She looked beautiful with her long, glossy brown hair. Dean would probably love to ask her out, if he could.

"What in the world happened, Bailey? Kit texted me and told me you just had an emotional car wreck, and I'm the only one you can talk to about it."

Bailey picked up her cupcake and took a big bite before answering. "She's right. If Taryn or Rob find out, I'll just die."

Jane frowned and crossed her legs as Kit brought her over a drink and a sandwich. "Eat this. You're going to need it," Kit said, before walking back to the counter.

Jane took a big bite of her cranberry, turkey and Gouda croissant, before motioning with her hand. "I've taken a bite. Now, tell me, before I die of curiosity."

Bailey sighed and then told Jane everything. From the very beginning to the very last word Dean said, and then sat back feeling exhausted and empty.

Jane stared at her in stunned silence. "Are you kidding me? He *really* said that? He wasn't joking, was he?"

Bailey shook her head sadly. "No, he wasn't joking. And now that I look back on everything, I should have picked up on all the signals he was putting out, but I just didn't want to see them, you know. I wanted my fantasy. I didn't want to accept that the man I was with, was constantly checking out other women. Heck, he's practically half way in love with Wren as it is. I hope Rob punches him in the nose, when he asks her out," she said, and then sat up with a gasp. "*Oh, no.* When he asks out Wren, she'll tell Rob and then he'll know, and then he'll be furious, and this will be an even bigger disaster."

Jane frowned and sat forward. "What could be worse than what we already have here?"

Bailey stared at Jane bleakly. "My mom finding out after I *just* told her yesterday that Dean was my boyfriend. That, and I told her he'd come to dinner on Sunday," she said, in a small scared voice.

Jane winced and patted her hand. "We'll come up with something, Bailey. Let's just keep things under wraps for a while, until you get a handle on things and figure out what to do. Kit and I won't say a word, but you might want to give Wren a heads up, in case Dean does go by to ask her out. Tell her not to tell Rob yet. She won't tell on you. Wren's a sweetheart."

Bailey nodded morosely. "Dean agrees. He thinks she's beautiful and a very talented chef as well."

Jane sighed and stood up. "Forget about him. I want you to go home, take a long hot bubble bath, and then watch something funny and eat some ice cream. Tomorrow is a new day. You can't let Dean have too much power over you. Okay?"

Bailey stood up and grabbed her trash, throwing it away before turning back to Jane. "How could a man I dated only a few times, have the power to crush me like this?"

Jane put her arm around Bailey's shoulder, as she walked her to the door. "Because in your mind, he was the man you'd been waiting for. You let your hope go wild and free, and now that it's been crushed, it hurts. But not for long. Feel it today. Own it. But then, be done with it."

Bailey nodded and opened the door. "Thanks for coming to talk to me, Jane. You're a good friend."

Jane nodded her head. "Of course, I came for you. You needed me."

Bailey walked down to her car and did as she was told. She drove home and turned the water on for a hot bubble bath. She popped the bubbles as they pushed up out of the water toward her and couldn't help comparing her relationship to the bubbles surrounding her. Full of rainbows and pretty, but weak and empty. Just like her relationship with Dean.

Chapter Eight

THE CONFESSION

The next day, Bailey glanced around the restaurant fearfully, hoping Dean hadn't made his move yet. She eased around the wall and studied the people eating and laughing. She felt her heart slow down, as she realized Dean wasn't there.

"Did you want a table Bailey, or are you eating with Taryn tonight?" Brittany asked, standing at her elbow.

Bailey jumped and turned to smile at the cute bubbly hostess. "Uh, no. Actually, I'm just going to head back and talk to Wren. About, um . . . the wedding. I just have a question for her."

Brittany smiled and gestured with her hand. "Tuesday's are kind of slow. She'll love to see you. Head on back and tell her that I overheard a couple leaving just now, and they couldn't stop raving about her food."

Bailey smiled easily and nodded. "Will do. Thanks, Brittany."

Bailey didn't wait to hear what else Brittany had to say, as she hurried down the hallway and past the crowded dining room, and to the back of the restaurant. She swiveled her head back and forth, keeping an eye out for Rob. If he found out, she'd die of humiliation. He'd find out eventually, but not today. Please, not today.

She pushed through the kitchen door and was immediately

engulfed with delicious and mouthwatering smells. She paused and closed her eyes, breathing in a lungful of heaven.

"Bailey! Just the girl I wanted to see. Come taste this," Wren called, from the stove.

Bailey smiled and walked over, leaning over to see what looked like a soup. "What is it?"

Wren dipped a spoon and lifted it to her lips. "Cauliflower soup with lobster. What do you think? I like to experiment on Tuesdays and tweak it so it's perfect by the weekend."

Bailey closed her eyes and concentrated on the flavors. She tasted the cauliflower and lobster, but she also tasted peas, corn and a touch of garlic. Amazing.

She opened her eyes and grinned. "Delicious. I love it, because it's not heavy, although it looks like it would be. It's light and fresh and the lobster really shines. You've done it again, Wren. Has Rob tasted it?"

Wren smiled in delight and shook her head. "I was actually getting ready to take him a bowl and get his opinion, but I'm feeling more confident now that I've seen your reaction. Kam told me it was a winner, but he says that about everything."

Bailey glanced around the kitchen and knew Kam was on break. "Well, probably because everything you make is delicious. Listen, Wren, I didn't come back here to sneak a free sample, I kind of need to talk to you about something. It's important."

Wren frowned and glanced around. "As soon as Kam comes back from break, I can take one with you. I haven't eaten yet and we can sit down and grab some dinner. Kam should be back in about ten minutes. He left to go check on his mom. She's been sick and he wanted to take her some soup."

Bailey smiled. "Wow, how sweet. Kam's a good son."

Wren nodded her head. "Kam's a good everything. Kindest man I know. Besides Rob, of course," she said, with a laugh. "Do me a favor. Take a bowl of this to Rob for me, and then I'll have more time to talk to you."

Bailey bit her lip but nodded her head. "Okay, good idea."

Wren filled a large bowl with soup and then grabbed two slices of sourdough bread to go with it. "Watch his reactions for me. Don't pay attention to what he says, but watch his face. Tell me what his eyes do when he takes the first bite."

Bailey laughed and picked up the bowl. "You're obsessed, Wren. Facial expressions?"

Wren blushed and pushed her out the kitchen door. "You're the same way with your writing and you know it."

Bailey shrugged. She had a point. Whenever someone created something, it was like they put a piece of their souls out into the world. It took a lot of bravery sometimes. She concentrated on not spilling the soup and wished she had some of the balance that Brogan had. She knocked on Rob's door and pushed it open with her hip. Rob saw her and grinned as he finished a conversation on the phone.

"Bailey! I was just thinking about you. Come in and have a seat. What did you bring me?"

Bailey carefully set the bowl down in front of him and watched his face light up. "Cauliflower and lobster soup. It's a new recipe."

Rob closed his eyes and took a deep breath. "It smells incredible. I love it when she creates new recipes. Makes life worth living," he murmured, before taking a big bite and closing his eyes the same way she had done.

Bailey did as she was told, and watched Rob's expressive face. He was already smiling so that was a good sign. When he finally opened his eyes he had that look on his face. The home run look. Total joy.

Bailey laughed and crossed her legs. "I take it you like it?"

Rob took another bite before answering. "It's like a dance of flavors in my mouth. *Mmmm*, and that hint of garlic just sets off the lobster. She's an artist."

Bailey nodded in total agreement. "You're a lucky man," she said softly, thinking of how much Dean liked Wren too.

Rob frowned at Bailey, as he took another bite. "Sis, what's wrong? You look so sad."

Bailey looked down at her lap and wished Rob wouldn't be so kind to her. She forced the sudden pressure of tears back and cleared her throat. "Rob, I'm fine. Just tired. Tell me how all the wedding preparations are coming? Did you two decide on where the reception will be?"

Rob studied his sister silently for a moment, and shook his head. "Something's up and you're not telling me, Bailey. You know I hate that. If I don't know, how can I help you?"

Bailey groaned and rubbed her temples, as she thought about just giving in and telling Rob everything. He might say, *I told you so*, but he'd also give her a hug and be on her side, no matter what.

"Rob, I can't tell you right now. It hurts too much. Can you just be patient with me, please? I just can't," she said softly, not looking at him.

Rob's face darkened and he pushed the soup away as he stared at his sister. "Something has hurt you that badly, and you won't tell me?"

Bailey sniffed back a tear and nodded silently. Rob sighed loudly and shook his head. "Fine, I'll give you two days tops, but then I want to know and I want to know everything."

Bailey wiped a little moisture from under her eyes and tried to smile. "I'll tell you when I can, okay?"

Rob nodded, his eyes dark and worried. "Okay, honey. When you can. Have you had dinner yet? You look like you could use a little dinner."

Bailey smiled and gestured toward the kitchen. "I'm actually going to take a break with Wren in a few minutes. I'll eat with her."

Rob stood up and motioned with his hands. "Come here and let me give you a hug. At least, let me do that."

Bailey stood up and hoped she didn't burst into tears on her big brother's shoulder. "Of course."

Rob wrapped his strong arms around her and held her gently for a moment before kissing her on top of her head. "Two days."

Bailey nodded jerkily and practically ran out of his office, breathing unsteadily. She paused before going back into the kitchen, and rested her head against the cool wall. She could do this. She could explain to Wren about Dean and beg for her cooperation. Easy. In and out. No emotion. Just facts. Wren would agree and then she could retreat back to her apartment and watch *Anne with an E* on Netflix.

She took a breath and stood up, pasting on a friendly smile, and then pushed through the kitchen door. She stopped in mid-stride as Kam turned and looked at her over his shoulder. He smiled at her, his flirty brown eyes lighting up, and she felt like crying again for some reason. *Wow*, she was a mess.

"Hey, Kam. Mind if I steal Wren away for a bit?" she asked breezily, as Wren caught sight of her and whipped her apron off with a flourish.

"Don't mind at all. Take your time. She needs to get off her feet."

Bailey smiled and nodded her head. "How's your mom? Wren said she wasn't feeling well."

Kam's smile widened and he turned to look at her fully. "You're asking about my mom? That's sweet. She's doing okay. She had a fever yesterday and today, so I thought some of Wren's soup would help her get her strength back."

Bailey smiled as Wren put her arm through hers. "I'm glad to hear it. Tell her I said, hi."

Kam nodded and watched her as Wren led her out of the kitchen. She could practically feel the weight of his eyes on her back. Wren seemed unaware of the undercurrents between her and Kam, and talked blithely about the wedding coming up. She and Rob were planning on a June wedding next month, and they were running out of time. Rob wanted to go overboard on everything and Wren kept fighting for a small, intimate reception.

"I just don't see why we can't have the reception here at the restaurant. It's the perfect size and Rob knows I hate big crowds. You have to talk to him, Bailey. He always listens to you. He thinks we should have the party of the century, but I swear if he does, I'm going to hide in the bathroom the entire time."

Bailey laughed as they found a table for two and sat down. She watched Wren sigh tiredly and frowned. "Kam's right. You do need a good break. You're working too hard, Wren."

Wren waved her hand in the air. "I love what I do. Now, tell me what's going on? I've never seen your eyes so sad before. You look like you just lost your best friend."

Brogan walked up then with two bowls of Wren's new soup and a side of truffle cream mac and cheese for Bailey. "Kam said you loved this and wanted you to have it. Jason will bring you over some drinks in a minute. Enjoy, ladies," he said, and rushed back to his own tables.

Wren took a bite of soup and smiled. "That was sweet of Kam to remember how much you loved the Mac and Cheese."

Bailey blushed a little and nodded. "Yeah, that was kind of thoughtful. Um, what I wanted to talk to you about, is kind of a private matter. It's actually really embarrassing and sort of humiliating too. And I really need you to *um*, keep it a secret for a while, until I can figure everything out. Can you do that?"

Wren's smile faded as she looked at Bailey and shook her head. "You want me to keep something humiliating a secret, from your family? Bailey, if something sad and embarrassing has happened to you, then your family needs to know. They love you so much. They'd kill any dragon for you. Heck, if Rob even thought you were holding something back from him, it would eat him alive."

Bailey groaned and took a bite of the mac and cheese and felt the instant comfort of the warm, cheesy and fragrant noodles. "Wow, this is so good. Um, well yeah. You're right about Rob, but I told him I would tell him in a couple days. He kind of took one look at me and knew something was up. But until then, would you please just help me out?"

Wren frowned but nodded her head. Jason, a new waiter from last summer who had dark spiky, black hair and a bright white smile, brought their water glasses and then disappeared almost as fast as Brogan had.

"I will. Of course, I will, unless I think you're in danger or something, and then I wouldn't be able to keep it a secret."

Bailey snorted and shook her head. "Yesterday, I had lunch with Dean and he told me that he plans on dating as many women as possible during the next year, and then at the end, he's going to pick the very best one."

Wren's mouth fell open and she sat back in her chair, stunned. "But, he's your boyfriend! You told us he was your boyfriend."

Bailey nodded her head and felt sick to her stomach. "I did. You're right, I spouted off about having a boyfriend, and I even bragged about it to my mother."

Wren groaned with her in commiseration and shook her head. "Oh, Bailey, that is horrible. But why do you need me to keep all of this a secret? I mean, I feel honored that you would tell me, but is there something else?"

Bailey blushed and took a bite of soup, to put off the moment for just a few seconds longer. "Dean admitted to me that he thinks you're beautiful and talented, and that he wants to ask you out. He wants you to join the harem, I guess. I was kind of worried that he had already come by. I figured if he did, and Rob found out, then life would kind of be, you know. *Over.*"

Wren's eyes were large and her face was lax, as if she couldn't take it in. "Didn't you tell Dean, I was engaged to your brother?"

Bailey shrugged and took a bite of the mac and cheese. "I mentioned a few times how much Rob loved you, but I guess Dean assumed that was in a professional capacity. I don't think he knows. So, when he comes by, just blow him off and maybe don't tell Rob?" she asked, wincing at what she was asking Wren to do.

Wren frowned and shook her head. "No, Bailey, I can't do

that. If Dean asks me out, of course, I'll have to tell Rob, but I'm so sorry, Bailey. I'm so sorry Dean didn't turn out to be the man you thought he was. Are you okay?"

Bailey nodded her head jerkily and tried to smile. "Great. Really great. I'm doing pretty good. I mean, it's not like we dated very long. I mean, yeah, it came as a shock to me. I have to admit, I fell pretty hard for him. He was kind of perfect for me, you know? So, yeah, it hurts, but I'm okay."

Wren nodded and reached over and grabbed Bailey's hand. "I'm going to make you a chocolate soufflé tomorrow, when you come in. Just for you. It's the best cure for heartbreak in the world."

Bailey smiled and rested her chin on her clasped hands. "Thanks, Wren, but could you please not tell Taryn or my mom? Rob would never rat me out, I guess, but I know how people gossip when they work in a restaurant, and I just don't want the whole world to know and have it get back to Taryn and my mom. *Please?*"

Wren frowned and took a bite of soup. "Well, now that I'm forewarned, if I see Dean trying to talk to me, I'll make sure no one overhears. I'll keep a lid on this, Bailey."

Bailey sighed in relief and let her shoulders fall, feeling all the tension she'd been carrying all day, go. "Oh, thank you, Wren. I'll try and steer Rob toward a small reception to pay you back."

Wren winced and took a sip of water. "It's hard, huh? Falling for the wrong guy. You feel so empty and embarrassed and stupid, don't you?"

Bailey nodded tiredly. "That describes it perfectly."

"Well, then you'll be relieved to know, that when you fall for the right guy, you're going to feel whole and light and brilliant and amazing. This will all be forgotten soon, Bailey. Rob and I and Taryn, we've all made mistakes when it comes to love. You have to know we'll stand by you. The only problem I see, really, is Anne. You told her you have a boyfriend, and you did say he was coming for dinner on Sunday. Maybe you could just tell her the truth? Explain it to her, just like you explained it to me. She's a reasonable woman. She'll be okay."

Bailey stared at Wren as if she were insane. "Have you met, Anne Downing?"

Wren grinned and nodded her head. "I have had that pleasure, yes. And she loves you, Bailey. That woman hurts when you hurt and she's happy when you're happy. It'll be okay."

Bailey shook her head quickly. "She'll hunt Dean down and demand to know, why he doesn't love me. She'll tell him off in front of all of his clients, or business associates and then he'll sue me. *No*, I'm putting this off, as long as I can. There has to be another solution."

Wren bit her lip and glanced around the restaurant. "You could bring a different man to dinner? You know, kind of distract her, so she doesn't focus on the lack of Dean."

Bailey frowned and thought about it. "But then that just puts a new man in her sights, and there aren't too many people that can survive that kind of attention. I'm still surprised you did."

Wren laughed, but then sat up straight and looked a little nervous. Bailey looked at her curiously, as Wren kicked her foot under the table.

"Hey, Rob. Come sit with me and help me finish my soup," Wren said, scooting over.

Rob walked up right then and put his hand on Wren's shoulder, before smiling at Bailey. "You girls look like you're enjoying yourselves. Mind if I join you?" he asked.

Bailey licked her lips and nodded her head and Rob slid in beside Wren. Rob smiled at Bailey, as his eyes studied her worriedly. He leaned over and kissed Wren lightly and put his arm around her shoulder.

"I just got a call from your boyfriend, Dean Hogan. He wanted me to give him Wren's personal phone number. Care to tell me why?" he asked lightly.

Bailey choked on her soup and grabbed her napkin, as Wren

turned red and looked helpless. Rob looked between the two women and looked grim.

"I take it you know, then?" Rob said dryly.

Bailey sighed miserably and glanced at Wren. Wren shrugged and looked down at her soup, torn between brother and sister.

Bailey groaned, feeling the crushing humiliation surround her. "Dean has a pretty big crush on Wren. He thinks she's beautiful and talented and wants to ask her out," she said quickly, looking down at her lap, as her face turned bright red in embarrassment.

Rob was silent for so long, she finally looked up to see his face completely stone-like, and his eyes red and angry.

"*He told you that?*" he finally hissed out.

Bailey nodded her head and slumped down in her seat in defeat. "Yesterday afternoon. He told me he plans on dating as many women as possible and then he'll pick the best one at the end of the year. I guess I wasn't good enough for him to stop looking, although he thinks I'm beautiful and wonderful. Just not the *most* beautiful or the *most* wonderful," she said softly, feeling the pain well up again and crash around her.

Rob's jaw tightened and he glanced at Wren. Wren stared up at him miserably and he sighed, pulling her into his side. "What a mess. What are we going to do about Mom?"

Bailey laughed in misery and then did what she'd been fighting all day and burst into tears. Rob sighed and immediately got up and sat down next to her, pulling his sister into his arms and holding her tightly.

"He's not worth it, Sis. He's not. Guys like him are just in it for the hunt. It doesn't matter who they're with, it's all about finding someone around the corner who is better. Forget about him."

Bailey leaned her head against her brother's shoulder and nodded. "I'm trying, but you see, I did something really stupid. I kind of told everyone he was my boyfriend and Mom is expecting *my boyfriend* for dinner on Sunday. You know what

Mom is like. What am I going to do?" she asked, taking the napkin Wren held out to her.

Rob ran his hand through his hair, making it stand up in dark spiky tufts. "Crud, Bailey, I don't know. Let me think about it. We have a few days, right? But you should have told me. You tried to keep me in the dark on this, and that's not right. Never again, okay?"

Bailey grimaced and nodded. "Yeah, sorry. I was just so embarrassed."

Rob kissed her forehead and stood up, walking back to sit by Wren. "And I haven't humiliated myself before? Come on, remember who you're talking to. I was beat up in front of the girl I loved. You can't get more embarrassing than that."

Bailey laughed and nodded. He had a point. Wren cleared her throat and sat forward. "Bailey, I still say that if we distract your mom with someone else, she won't throw such a big fit over Dean. Maybe, just tell her that you were teasing her about having a boyfriend, but that you *are* starting to date more seriously now. Bring a cute guy to dinner and see what happens."

Rob smiled and nodded his head. "That would be perfect. What guy do you know, who could come to a Downing family dinner, and survive our mother?"

Bailey shrugged and shook her head. "We barely survive family dinners, and we're Downings. No one, Rob. No one I'd want to ever date again. That's the thing about family dinners and meeting mothers. It's not so casual. What kind of guy would do that and still be able to be a casual friend with me?"

Rob's face fell and he grabbed her bowl of mac and cheese, taking a big bite. "Well, when you put it that way, no one."

Wren shook her head and drummed her hands on the table. "I know someone who would."

Rob and Bailey stopped eating and turned to stare at Wren. "Not possible," Bailey said.

Wren grinned and smiled widely. "Kam Matafeo could take

on your mother any day of the week *and* have her eating out his hand the entire time."

Rob's face lit up and he kissed Wren loudly. "Baby, you're a genius. Kam would be perfect. What do you think, Bailey? We could tell him what happened and he'd love to help you out. He's always gone out of his way to be nice to you."

Bailey turned green at the thought of telling Kam about her humiliation. "*No,* never. No way. *Uh uh,*" she muttered, shaking her head quickly. "No, no, no."

Rob frowned and Wren looked crestfallen. "Oh, well I thought it was the perfect solution," Wren said, in confusion.

Rob narrowed his eyes as he stared at her. "*Ah,* I get it. Okay, no pressure. Listen, I gotta get back to the office, so I'll let you girls finish your dinner. Call me tomorrow, okay, Bailey?" he asked, in a way that made it sound more like an order.

Bailey nodded and smiled. Wren grabbed Rob's hand before he could walk away. "Hey, what did you tell Dean, when he asked for my number?"

Rob grinned, looking like a naughty little boy for a second. "I might have told him to never come near my restaurant again, my sister again, or my future wife again."

Wren frowned and Rob laughed as he walked away. Bailey sighed and looked down at her half eaten meal. "Well, I guess it's okay that Rob knows, but no one else, Wren. Okay?"

Wren nodded and stood up. "Of course, not. I've gotta get back to the kitchen, but stay and finish up. You look thinner than usual. He's not worth it, you know."

Bailey nodded her head and waved her off. She stared around the restaurant at all of the couples sitting together eating and laughing and felt a little bitter. That was her just last week. Happy.

Chapter Nine

KAM'S CONFUSION

Saturday morning, Bailey was desperate. She sat on her couch with her laptop and stared at all of her Facebook contacts, skimming through all the men she knew. She gave up and switched to Instagram. There had to be somebody.

She'd gotten a text from Wren an hour ago. Just one word. *Kam.* She flipped through her friends a second time and then finally gave up, shutting the laptop and leaning back to stare at her ceiling. There had to be a solution, besides going to Kam for help. She could just imagine his face now. The surprise, the pity and then the interest that was always there. He'd feel sorry for her, but then he'd see it as an opportunity to get closer to her, and that just made her too nervous. She wasn't up to handling Kam Matafeo. He was just too much of everything. Too big, too handsome, too nice. Too perfect.

And she, Bailey Downing, was so far from perfect, that it wasn't even funny. She sighed and pushed the laptop off her lap. She'd promised Rob she'd be at his rugby game in an hour, so she had an hour to eat breakfast and get ready. Jane couldn't come that morning, because she was babysitting for Layla and Michael, so she'd agreed to pick up the cupcakes and hot chocolate and bring them to the game.

She rushed through her shower and threw on what was closest. An old WSU t-shirt, skinny jeans and her black hiking boots. She twisted all of her blond hair into a high messy bun and spent only a minute high-lighting her eyes. She rolled her eyes at her reflection in the mirror and smiled cynically. If Dean could see her now, she'd be dropped from the top ten for sure. She grabbed her keys and ran out the door, glancing at the clock. She was late. She hurried over to the bakery and loaded the boxes of cupcakes and the cooler of hot chocolate, hugged Jane and then rushed to the field. She winced at all the cars and the people already on the field. She hated being late.

It took her two trips, but she got everything set up by the time the first time out was called. Wren ran up, just as she handed the first cup of hot chocolate out, and Bailey raised an eyebrow.

"You are so late. Does Rob know what a rotten girlfriend you are?" she asked teasingly.

Wren laughed and pushed a stray lock of long strawberry blond hair out of her eyes. "It's Rob's fault I'm late. He insisted on taking me dancing last night, and we stayed out too late. Oh, Bailey, we had so much fun. There is nothing like dancing with the man you love," she said, in a soft voice, before she was picked up from behind and twirled around.

Bailey grinned at her brother as he kissed his fiancée in front of everyone, embarrassing Wren so much, she turned bright red. "Have a cupcake, Rob and stop embarrassing my friend."

Rob laughed and set Wren down, so he could take a cup of hot chocolate. "She's not embarrassed. She's in love. *Right?*"

Wren leaned up and kissed him on the cheek and nodded. "I am," she said, so honestly and directly, that Rob paused and stared down at Wren. Bailey cleared her throat, feeling embarrassed herself that she was witnessing such a simple but beautiful moment between two people.

"You two, knock it off. You know Bailey hates public displays of affection. Makes her twitchy."

Bailey turned around and frowned up at Kam. "I am not twitchy! Why would you say that?" she asked, feeling grumpy all of a sudden.

Kam took the cup of hot chocolate she handed to him, and put his arm around her shoulders. "Because every time I try to show you a little affection, you run in the opposite direction," he said dryly.

Bailey swallowed nervously. "Have a cupcake," she said lamely, trying to shift the conversation.

Rob walked over and pounded Kam on the back. "That last tackle you made was epic, Kam. I swear you were flying. I can't believe you didn't play professional football."

Kam laughed and let his arm drop from Bailey's shoulder as he picked up a cupcake. "I played for WSU, but it wasn't for me."

Rob blinked in surprise. "Seriously? Why didn't you go pro? Even if it wasn't your thing, playing for even a few years would have set you up financially for the rest of your life."

Kam shook his head and took another sip. "I didn't like who I was when I played football. It wasn't worth it to me."

Bailey stood back and listened to their conversation and couldn't stop the feeling of admiration she was experiencing for Kam. She stared at him as he talked to her brother and wished for a moment that she could have been a different woman. A woman who wasn't so afraid. A woman who was brave enough to be with a man like Kam.

Kam glanced at her and caught her eyes. What he saw on her face must have surprised him, because his eyes widened and he smiled slowly at her. Bailey blinked out of the trance she was in and looked away quickly. Of course, Kam would catch her daydreaming about him. With her luck, she only had a few more embarrassing moments to go, to reach her daily quota.

"Bailey, they can pour their own hot chocolate. I've gotta talk to you," Wren said, putting her arm through hers and pulling her away from the team.

Bailey sighed in relief and followed her gratefully. Even standing in the same vicinity as Kam was dangerous. "What's up?"

Wren stared at her with a raised eyebrow. "What do you mean, what's up? *You're* up. Tomorrow's dinner at your mom's house is what's up. Bailey, what are you going to do? Let me talk to Kam and I swear that man will do anything in his power to help you."

Bailey glanced back over her shoulder and looked at Kam, who was now standing at an angle to Rob. The perfect position to be looking at her, while he carried on a conversation. Their eyes met and his eyes darkened, as his smile grew wider. Bailey bit her lip and turned back to Wren.

"No Wren. *No*. Please, let it go. I've been looking through all my contacts and all the guys I've been out with, and half of them are married now, or engaged or expecting babies. I think I'm just going to have to face the fire tomorrow on my own," she said weakly, feeling sick just thinking about it.

Wren frowned and shook her head. "Have you met Anne Downing?"

Bailey laughed and nodded her head. "We all have. And there ... *she is* ... right now," she said in shock, as she watched her mother walk toward them wearing a large sweatshirt and carrying a camping chair. "She never comes to Saturday games."

Wren turned slowly around and put on a bright smile, waving her hand in the air. "You can do this, Bailey. Just smile and change the subject anytime it gets weird, okay?"

Bailey nodded and smiled brightly as Anne Downing joined them, looking happier than she'd looked in a long time.

"There are my girls! Where's Taryn? We could have a family reunion right here, couldn't we?" she asked, with a loud laugh, waving at Rob.

Bailey bit her lip as the whistle blew and all the men ran back out onto the field.

"So, where's Dean, Bailey? Didn't you invite him to your

brother's game? I think it's important that family is a priority. You know that."

Bailey winced and shoved her hands in to her pockets. "Dean, um is busy, Mom, but I'm surprised to see you here. You never come to Saturday games."

Anne fluffed her poofy hair and smiled. "I don't know, I just have all of this extra energy these days. I think it's because I'm so happy. Wren and Rob getting married next month is a dream come true, but to know that my baby is in love, has given me so much joy, I just don't know what to do with myself. I joined a bowling league this week, can you believe it? I feel so alive again. Life is perfect. Well, it would be if Taryn found love too, but I'm content."

Wren turned her body and stared at Bailey with wide eyes. Bailey swallowed and looked away. Her mom was bowling now. Could life get any worse?

Wren did her best to distract Anne with talk about food for Sunday dinner while Bailey racked her brain for a solution to her problem. Her eyes kept straying to Kam and she wondered if maybe she should ask him? Her mother's future bowling trophies were at stake.

When the whistle blew, Rob bounded over, picking his mom up in his arms and hugged her tightly, making her squawk and giggle. "Robert, put me down this instant or you're grounded," she said laughingly, and even Bailey grinned at that.

Kam walked up to the group and smiled down at her. "Thanks for cheering for me. I heard you yelling my name."

Bailey reddened and pushed a stray wisp of hair out of her eyes. "Well, that was an amazing tackle."

Kam grinned and casually put an arm around Bailey's shoulders. Rob, Wren and Anne turned as one to look at Bailey, and Bailey blushed as her mom stared at Kam's hand on her daughter's shoulder. Anne's eyes widened and she looked at Bailey with a raised eyebrow. Bailey looked away and bit her lip. Wren cleared her throat as Rob smiled happily.

"So, I take it Kam is coming then?" Rob asked, looking relieved.

Bailey groaned softly as Kam looked down at her curiously. "Coming to what?"

Anne frowned and stepped closer to her daughter. "It's Kam, right? You work for my son at the restaurant?"

Kam nodded his head, still looking back and forth between Rob and Bailey. "I do. I'm Wren's sous chef. And you must be Rob and Bailey's mother. It's a pleasure to meet you. I've heard nothing but wonderful things about you."

Anne relaxed immediately as Kam reached out a hand to shake hers and smiled happily. "Well, that's so sweet. I've heard from Wren and Rob what an amazing cook you are. Wren told me just the other day, that she wouldn't be able to do what she does if it weren't for you. She said she'd fall apart without you."

Kam grinned at Wren and winked at her. "Well, don't believe it. Wren's a little whirlwind and she'd probably do just fine without me."

Wren and Rob started talking on top of each other, complimenting Kam, and Bailey laughed as they tried to outdo each other. Kam grinned and stepped back, putting his arm back around her shoulders. Anne noticed immediately and looked confused.

"So, it looks like you know Bailey too. How exactly do you two know each other?" she asked, glancing back at Rob with an arched eyebrow.

Bailey cleared her throat and glanced up at Kam. Kam smiled warmly down at her, waiting to see what she would say. "Kam and I are friends, Mom. We know each other from the restaurant of course."

Anne nodded her head and glanced at Kam's arm one more time. "Oh, well that's good then. Does *Dean* know Kam?" she asked.

Kam frowned and looked down at her. Bailey closed her eyes and sighed. Might as well just get all of the humiliation over with now. She opened her mouth to speak, but was interrupted by Rob.

"Mom, Bailey dumped Dean last week. She's already started dating someone else," Rob said, smiling at Anne.

Bailey let out a large breath and stared at her feet. *Who was she dating now?* Ugh, Rob!

Anne frowned darkly and crossed her arms over her chest, a sure sign that an impromptu family council was getting ready to begin. "*Who,* Rob? *Who* is Bailey dating?" she demanded, looking almost angry.

Wren stared at Bailey and tilted her head toward Kam. Bailey shook her head quickly in the negative. She couldn't drag Kam into her drama. It would be too embarrassing and too . . . *dangerous.*

Wren cleared her throat and smiled brightly. "She's been dating Brogan, of course. You know Brogan, Anne. Good looking, blond guy who works for Rob? He's the best waiter we have. He's paying off his college loans, while he starts his graphic design business. Really smart guy and Rob loves him like a brother. He's coming to dinner tomorrow, right Bailey?"

Bailey's mouth fell open in shock as Rob, Anne and Kam turned to stare at her in surprise. Kam's dark, brown eyes, usually filled with light and playfulness, darkened dangerously and he slowly removed his hand from her shoulder. Bailey immediately missed the comforting weight of his hand.

"Brogan. *Yes,* um . . . Brogan is a great guy," she said lamely. A great guy who happened to be in love with her sister, Taryn.

Kam stepped back from her and looked down at her suspiciously. "When did you start dating Brogan, Bailey? I think I would have noticed that," he said dryly.

Bailey couldn't meet his eyes and shoved her hands in her jean pockets. Wren jumped in to save her. "It's a new thing, Kam. You know Bailey, she's not the type to go on and on about her love life."

Kam nodded his head once and sighed. "No, you're right. She

isn't. Have fun tomorrow at your family dinner," he said, in a toneless voice that had Bailey staring at him. Their eyes collided and she saw shock, disappointment and yearning.

Kam turned and walked away without another word and Rob moved to fill in the gap, putting his arm around Bailey's shoulder. "Bailey, do you remember that favor I asked you to do for me? Back at the restaurant? Could you take care of that now? I know you'll have to miss the rest of the game, but it's really important to me."

Bailey looked up at Rob with gratitude in her eyes. "I totally remember, Rob. I would never let you down. I'll have to hurry though. Bye, Mom, bye, Wren," she said quickly, and hugged Rob hard, before running toward the parking lot.

Rob was getting the biggest birthday present in the world this year. No one could have a better brother than she did. She reached her car and jumped in, taking a moment to lean her head against the steering wheel.

She was dating Brogan. *Thanks to Wren's imagination*, she was now dating Brogan. Now, to tell Brogan that. She turned on her car and caught site of Kam running back onto the field. Kam hadn't looked too happy at that news. She couldn't wait to see what Taryn's reaction was going to be. Bailey sat up and smiled a little. That part might actually be fun. A new idea formed in Bailey's head and a gleeful smile lit up her face. She was going to kill two birds with one stone with Brogan. She was going to save herself, and maybe push Taryn out of her comfort zone.

Chapter Ten

BROGAN'S HEART

Bailey got to the restaurant just as Taryn was finishing up with the wait staff. She waved at Taryn and Taryn nodded her head at her. A minute later, everyone scattered and began their preparations for the day, setting the tables and polishing glasses. Taryn walked over and hugged her.

"What's going on? You looked stressed out."

Bailey widened her eyes innocently and smiled brightly. "I'm good! Super good. Like, amazingly good," she added, since her sister looked so doubtful.

Taryn laughed and shook her head. "Well, I guess so, since you're bringing your new boyfriend to dinner tomorrow. Come on, let's go back to my office and you can show me his picture on your phone again."

Bailey blushed at the reminder of cell phone shrine to Dean, and shook her head. "Actually, I'm here to talk to Brogan, but I'll stop by before I go," she said, and turned to walk away, hoping Taryn didn't pull her back and grill her.

Taryn pulled her back. "*What?* Why do you want to talk to Brogan?" she asked, with a frown.

Bailey shrugged and tried to look innocent. "Well, things actually didn't work out between me and Dean. I deleted my shrine a few days ago. I'm kind of thinking about going for Brogan to be honest. He's gorgeous, sweet, smart and strangely available. I might as well go for it, right?" she asked, studying Taryn's reaction. "And hey, if it gets Mom off my back, why not?"

Taryn stood where she was, completely still as if she were frozen. No reaction whatsoever. Bailey frowned in disappointment. She had been hoping that Taryn would show *something*. Taryn finally blinked, and gave her a stiff smile.

"Oh, I had no idea that you liked Brogan like that. I, *ah* . . . thought you two were just friends."

Bailey shrugged. "Friendship can turn into love. That's what you always tell me, right?"

Taryn's face looked pinched for a moment, but she smiled and even laughed a little. "Too right. Stop by before you go."

Bailey nodded and waved as she walked away. Taryn hadn't looked thrilled. Maybe that was the best reaction she could hope for. She found Brogan going over the menu, as he drank a glass of ice water.

"Hey, gorgeous! What brings you my way this beautiful spring day?" he asked, his blue eyes kind and curious.

Bailey blushed a little and then leaned in toward him, so no one could accidentally overhear. "I have a proposition for you."

Brogan raised an eyebrow and put the menu down, stepping closer to her. "Why does this sound so R-rated?"

Bailey laughed and grabbed Brogan's arm as she leaned up to whisper in his ear. "You're not wrong. I want you to come to my mom's house for dinner and pretend to be interested in me. In return, I'll help you wake up my sister to the fact that *she's* very interested in you."

Brogan's eyes lit up and he stared down at her as a large smile lit his face. "She already knows she's interested in me. The problem is, she doesn't want to be."

Bailey frowned and tapped her chin. "How about you and I work together as a team, to maneuver Taryn into a corner, so that she has to admit that she has feelings for you? Feelings, that I personally think, she's been fighting for years now."

Brogan closed his eyes and shook his head. "You are the answer to my prayers. And all I have to do is come to a family dinner? I'm there. Do you want flowers? Candy? Name it and it's yours."

Bailey jumped up and down as relief poured through her. *She was saved.* "I love you, I love you, I love you!" she yelled, before jumping into Brogan's arms. Brogan laughed and held her tightly, before setting her down. He cleared his throat and she glanced around to notice that every single waiter and waitress was staring at them with their mouths open. A few waitresses looked heart-broken. She bit her lip and grinned.

"Sorry!" she called out to everyone. "Brogan kind of makes me lose control sometimes," she added, noting that one waitress looked very close to tears. She leaned in close to Brogan and whispered, "Check out the blond. I think you just broke her heart."

Brogan sighed in relief. "And for that, I'll do anything you ask of me."

Bailey grinned. "Okay, this is how it'll play. I'll pick you up and we'll drive over to my mom's at one. You act like you're smitten with me and I'll act like I'm smitten with you. My mom will not have an emotional breakdown because I'm not there with Dean, and we'll drive Taryn crazy at the same time. She'll throw her plate of crab cakes at me in a rage and drag you off to the family room, where she'll declare her passionate love for you. My mom will be grateful one of her daughters has found love, and I'll be able to ride off into the sunset, happy and free from family obligations. What do you think?"

Brogan had a dreamy look in his eyes as he smiled. "It sounds like the best Disney movie I've ever seen. If this works, Bailey, I swear I'll love you forever."

Bailey grinned, feeling euphoric and weightless after her week of misery. "Start loving me then, because this is done," she said, as Brogan picked her up in his arms and hugged her again.

"I didn't realize you two were so close."

Bailey felt her feet touch the ground and she turned around to see Kam standing before her, still wearing his rugby uniform and looking slightly murderous.

"Hey, man, looks like you guys won. Rob treating the team to gnocchi?" Brogan asked easily.

Kam nodded as a few more rugby players trickled into the restaurant behind him. "You and Bailey. When did this start?" he asked, ignoring Brogan's question.

Brogan caught onto Kam's displeasure and he glanced at Bailey quickly with a slight smile. "Oh, gotcha. Um, Bailey and I have always been close, but I'd have to say our relationship took a serious turn fairly recently. Wouldn't you say, Bailey?"

Bailey cleared her throat and clasped her hands in front of her. "Is there anyone who hasn't fallen in love with Brogan?" she asked, her voice squeaky and unsure sounding.

Kam glared at her and stepped closer. "You never did. You've known Brogan since you were a kid, and you never fell in love with him. What's going on, Bailey, because I don't buy this," he said, pointing to Brogan.

Brogan winced and pointed to the kitchen. "I'm going to bring out the platters of gnocchi. You two look like you need to talk," he said, and disappeared.

Kam stared at her and then grabbed her hand, pulling her down the hall to Rob's office. He pushed the door open and pulled her inside and then shut the door.

Bailey's mouth fell open and she put her hands on her hips. "What do you think you're doing?" she hissed. "You can't just drag me around, whenever you feel like it."

Kam's mouth tightened and he stepped closer to her. "First Dean and now Brogan? I'm sick of it, Bailey. You can't look at me the way you do and date everyone else. I'm not blind, Bailey. I see the way you look at me. You want me just as much as I want you, but you're too afraid to admit it. When are you going to be brave enough to admit that *I'm* the one you want, and stop looking for the perfect man to fit your perfect life and your perfect image? You don't look at Brogan, the way you look at me."

Bailey swallowed hard and felt as if the wind had been knocked out of her. "You don't know what you're talking about," she whispered.

Kam stepped closer, so that they were now knee to knee and he tilted her chin up with his finger. "I know you don't think I'm good enough for you. You look at me and see some guy with a tattoo and long hair, and you don't give me a chance. Then you bring some idiot wearing a suit here to dinner, and think he's the one for you. And when that doesn't work out, you settle for Brogan, a guy you treat like a brother. I'm done with whatever this is, Bailey. Stop torturing me," he ground out, and then pulled her into his arms and began kissing her.

Bailey had relived the kiss they'd shared at Taryn's birthday party over and over in her mind, but this kiss was so much more. Without even realizing what she was doing, she wrapped her arms around Kam's neck and went up on her tiptoes, angling her head and relaxing into the kiss in a way, she'd never been able to do before.

Kam didn't waste time and deepened the kiss, pushing her up against the door. When he finally pulled away, Bailey could barely stand up straight.

"That . . . *was* . . ." She was going to say amazing, but couldn't form the words with her mouth.

Kam stared at her grimly, his hands still around her waist. "You can't kiss me like that and deny that you have feelings for me. I won't let you."

Bailey licked her lips and leaned weakly against the door as she stared up into Kam's blazing, brown eyes. "Kam, this is complicated. I do . . . I *do* feel something when I look at you. But that doesn't mean that we would be good together."

Kam glared down at her and kissed her again. A few minutes later when he pulled her arms from around his neck he raised an eyebrow. "We'd be great together. Stop pushing me away, Bailey. I don't want to kill Brogan, but if you insist on dating him, I can't guarantee his safety."

Bailey surprised herself and laughed. She reached up and traced Kam's mouth with her finger and felt her stomach twist pleasantly. "It's all pretend, Kam. I'm taking him to dinner tomorrow to get my mom off my back. Dean didn't work out and she'll have a nervous breakdown thinking I'll never give her grandchildren. And I'm hoping it will push Taryn into admitting that she likes Brogan. I'm not doing it to hurt you. I'm just trying to survive my mom."

Kam frowned and captured her hand in his before kissing her palm. "Forget about making Taryn jealous and take me. I'm the one you belong with," he said softly, reaching down to kiss her neck.

Bailey felt her nerve endings jump for joy and had to restrain herself from jumping into his arms. "It's already set up for tomorrow, Kam. Don't be jealous. Honestly, there's no reason."

Kam stood up and let go of her hand as he stared down at her thoughtfully. "Are you going to walk out that door and pretend that you never kissed me? Are you going to keep me at arm's length?"

Bailey studied the large man standing in front of her, and felt a yearning she hadn't felt in a long time. A yearning to belong somewhere, *with someone*, who wanted to be with her and just her. She sighed as some of the old fears wrapped around her, trying to squeeze her heart.

"I don't want to, Kam, but when I look at you, I'm scared," she whispered.

Kam closed his eyes as if he were in pain. "I'd never hurt you, Bailey. *Ever.*"

Bailey reached out and touched his arm. "Not physically. Kam, you're the gentlest man I've ever known. But when I look at you, I just know that you'd take everything. You'd take all of me. And what would be left, when I look up one day and you're gone?"

Kam slowly raised his eyes and stared at her. "Stop being so scared of love, Bailey. Stop being scared of what you feel for me. Allow yourself to feel this connection between us."

Bailey shook her head and grasped her elbows. "It's not that easy, Kam. I've been . . . *hurt* before. I've been betrayed before. Loving you is the scariest thing I could ever do."

Kam reached out and touched her cheek. "No one would ever love you the way I could. Think about that while you're having dinner with Brogan tomorrow," he said, and then pulled her out of the way of the door and walked out, leaving her shaken and confused.

Chapter Eleven

DINNER WITH MOM

Bailey and Brogan pulled up to her mom's house right at one. She turned off her car and turned in her seat to look at Brogan. He looked perfect. Khaki's, a polo shirt and nice shoes. He looked like a Gap commercial, with his blond hair and strong attractive features.

"It's like you're perfect, Brogan. How do you live with yourself?"

Brogan laughed and angled the mirror toward her. "You're one to talk. Look at you. All that long blond hair, gorgeous, blue eyes and the face of a Brazilian model. I guess if you look at just the superficial, you and I do make the perfect couple."

Bailey grinned and shook her head. "And there you are, obsessed with my wild and beautiful older sister."

Brogan shrugged and looked away. "Opposites do attract, which is why there's a very large Samoan, who would love to tear me limb from limb right now. You really should stop torturing that guy, and go out with him."

Bailey frowned and pushed her hair over her shoulder. "I'm seriously thinking about it, actually. But enough about my love life. Let's focus on our game plane. Two things. Protect me from my mother and I'll do whatever I can to make Taryn jealous enough, that she'll be forced to admit that she likes you. Any questions?"

Brogan looked away as if he were uncomfortable.

"What? What's the matter, Brogan?" Bailey demanded, praying he wasn't getting ready to back out.

Brogan shrugged and closed his eyes. "How are you going to make Taryn jealous? I've tried to make her jealous a few times, with some of the waitresses. I'd flirt a little here and there, and she didn't have any reaction to it."

Bailey sighed and looked away. "Well, I'm her sister, so there's that. And I guess I'll just play it by ear. If she doesn't give us the reaction we want, I'll um, push the, uh . . . *limits* I guess," she said, in a small voice.

Brogan laughed and lifted an eyebrow. "Why do you look so ill? Come on, kissing me can't be that horrifying."

Bailey grinned and opened the door. "It's not horrifying, I'm just thinking of you in the hospital, when Kam finds out."

Brogan groaned and joined her on the sidewalk. "That's right, your Samoan, future significant other, could seriously hurt me. Just don't let him break my hands. I need those for my business."

Bailey patted him on the back as they walked up to the front door of the small rambler. "I'll make sure he concentrates on your face. Now, put your arm around me."

Brogan slipped his arm around her waist and brought her in close to his side, just as the door opened. Bailey blinked in surprise to see Wren.

"Hey, Wren," she said, relaxing and smiling. "I was expecting Mom."

Wren smiled and looked over her shoulder. "She's finishing up the garlic bread. Come on in, you two are the last to arrive," she said, with a small smile.

Bailey looked at her suspiciously and pulled Brogan inside. Brogan leaned down and kissed Wren on the cheek, before following her into the dining room. Bailey hurried to grab

Brogan's hand, so they could make a nice romantic entry for Taryn's sake.

They walked into the dining room to see Rob already seated, and Taryn looking cool and beautiful and . . . *Kam*. Bailey's mouth dropped open and she turned and stared at Wren. "What's he doing here?" she hissed, in Wren's ear.

Wren shrugged and whispered back. "I invited him."

Bailey glared at Wren's back, but quickly pasted on a smile, as she gestured to Brogan. "You all know Brogan, my um, *sweetie*."

aryn stared daggers at Brogan as they walked around the table so they could sit next to each other. Which meant, Kam would be sitting on her left and Brogan on her right. She smiled politely at Kam, as Brogan held her chair for her.

"Hi, Kam, what a surprise to see you here," she said lightly, as she placed the napkin on her lap.

Kam reached under the table and grabbed her hand in his. "Oh, I wouldn't miss it. Wren told me your mom is an amazing cook."

Bailey tried to pull her hand away, but couldn't. She kicked Kam in the shin, but he just smiled at her. She rolled her eyes and felt Brogan nudge her knee. She glanced over at him and remembered what she'd promised.

"Brogan, thanks for coming to dinner today. I never imagined you and I would be sitting together at a family dinner, but you know what, it feels right having you here."

Brogan grinned and took a sip of water. "It feels right to me, too. I've always felt like part of the Downing family."

Taryn stared at Brogan across the table as she tapped her fingers on the table. "How long have you liked my sister?" she demanded in a hard voice, that had Bailey's eyes going wide.

Brogan cleared his throat and put his arm over the back of Bailey's chair. "Bailey is a gorgeous woman. She's intelligent, kind and she's very perceptive about feelings. She doesn't care what other people think about the two of us being together. She puts my feelings for her first. I find that very attractive," he said softly, staring back at Taryn.

Kam snorted lightly, and Bailey glared at him, all the while Kam's thumb lightly caressed the top of her hand. He leaned over and whispered in her ear, "Do you care what other people think, Bailey? Does it bother you that people might look at you and me and not approve?"

Bailey glanced around the table, but Taryn and Brogan were busy glaring at each other and Rob and Wren had gotten up to help her mom bring the food out. She looked over at Kam, which was a mistake, because as soon as she did, she was caught by his big, brown eyes. She shook her head and leaned over to whisper in his ear, "Of course not, Kam. Don't you know me at all?"

Kam frowned and scooted his chair closer to hers and leaned down to her ear again. "Something is holding you back. Just tell me what it is."

Bailey bit her lip, and shook her head. "*Kam . . .*"

"*Ah!* Look at this, all three of my beautiful children and their dates. I couldn't be happier."

Bailey moved away from Kam and smiled brightly at her mom. "Mom, you remember Brogan Moore."

Anne set down the platter of garlic bread as she beamed at Brogan. "Of course, I do! You were always such a good looking boy, but I have to say, you've grown up to be a gorgeous man. You and Bailey look just like Ken and Barbie sitting there together."

Taryn snorted while Wren giggled and Bailey groaned. Rob walked in with a bowl of pasta and looked around at everyone's amused faces. "What did I miss?"

Wren pointed to Bailey and Brogan and laughed again. "Your mom just pointed out, that Bailey and Brogan look just like Ken and Barbie."

Rob tilted his head back and laughed at that, before sitting down next to Wren. "Oh, wow, that's sad."

Bailey glanced up at Kam and bit her lip. He was not smiling at all. Taryn noticed Kam's expression and cleared her throat. "Mom, you met Kam at the rugby game yesterday. Wren invited him to dinner because she thinks of him as her family. It's only right that he come to Sunday dinners with Wren."

Anne walked over and put her hands on Kam's shoulders. "Of course, he's welcome. Kam, my home is your home."

Kam grinned and looked up at Anne. "Thank you so much, Mrs. Downing. I appreciate your hospitality and your kindness."

Anne beamed and patted his shoulder one more time before taking her seat. "Call me, Anne, I insist. Rob, would you please say the prayer and we can begin."

Rob said a prayer over the food and began passing the bowls and platters around the table. Conversation was easy and upbeat and Bailey started to relax. The only person not having a good time, looked to be Taryn, who was unnaturally quiet and somber.

Bailey cleared her throat and smiled over at Rob. "Rob, I feel kind of guilty. Yesterday when I was giving Brogan a hug, a couple of your waitresses burst into tears. I hope you don't lose any wait staff, because Brogan is off the market."

Kam reached over and grabbed her hand at that, and she glanced at him quickly. He smiled at her, but there was a warning in his eyes, that made her blink in surprise. Taryn laughed, a hard, brittle sound, that didn't sound anything like Taryn's normal laugh.

"Brogan's been breaking hearts since he was sixteen. Right, Brogan? You're probably so used to it, you don't even notice anymore. Do you?" she asked quietly.

Brogan stared across the table at Taryn solemnly, before answering. "I notice. I notice, because I've had my heart broken. Not just once though. But over and over. I don't like causing anyone pain. Unlike some people," he said coldly.

Bailey watched curiously as her sister's cold eyes turned hot and dangerous. Rob must have noticed too, because he laughed lightly and handed Taryn a salad bowl. "I don't worry about Brogan. He's got a heart of gold. That's why so many women fall for him. Because there's so few men who are genuinely kind and good. I'm just glad one of my sisters was smart enough to fall for Brogan," he said dryly.

Brogan grinned at Rob and nodded his head. "Love you too, Rob."

Rob laughed and Anne beamed at her full dinner table. "Look at this. Every chair is filled. I don't know what I'll do when Rob and Wren start having children. I'll have to get a bigger table," she said, her eyes glowing at the thought.

Taryn groaned softly and stared at her plate, while Wren blushed and Rob grinned. "Mom, I'll get you a new table to fit all my children. I don't know what you'll do when Taryn and Bailey start having kids though."

Anne grinned at Rob and then glanced at Bailey. Bailey immediately began eating and tried to look innocent.

"Bailey, I'm so confused. You'll have to explain how just last week, some man named Dean was your boyfriend, and now you're dating Brogan. You must have had a busy week," she said, narrowing her eyes at her youngest daughter.

Brogan reached over and put his arm around Bailey's shoulder and smiled at Anne. "That was probably my fault, Anne. I take full responsibility. If there's not a ring on the finger, I say she's fair game."

Anne laughed and pounded her hand on the table. "Now, that's a man. Look at that, Taryn. You need a man like that. Someone who sees what he wants, and isn't afraid to go after it. I like you, Brogan. You'll do just fine."

Bailey glanced at Brogan quickly and smiled in gratitude, and he winked at her, just as Kam's hand slipped under the table and took possession of her hand, *again*. She whipped her head around and stared at Kam with warning in her eyes, but he was too mad to care. She could see something dangerous brewing in his eyes, and she smiled weakly at him.

"Kam," she said softly, begging him to not do or say anything to ruin their dinner. He narrowed his eyes at her, and she let out a nervous breath.

Taryn sat back and crossed her arms over her chest as she stared at Brogan. "Yeah, Brogan is a great guy. He'd be perfect, but he's just so young. You're what? Twenty-four?"

Brogan stared back at Taryn and nodded his head. "That's right Taryn, I'm twenty-four and you're twenty-seven. Three years older than me. Why is that *such* a *big* hang up for you?" he asked, in a hard voice.

Rob and Wren looked up and shared looks with Bailey, as they watched the byplay between Brogan and their sister.

Taryn rolled her eyes. "I was best friends with your older sister, Brogan. The first time I met you, you were *fourteen* and running around the backyard, playing with squirt guns."

Brogan grinned and sat back. "I remember that day as if it were yesterday. You and Kelly were sunbathing in the backyard. You were wearing a red bikini and you had on huge movie star sunglasses. I thought you were the most beautiful thing I'd ever seen in my life," he said softly.

Taryn blushed and looked away, while Rob and Bailey exchanged gleeful looks. Anne looked confused though. "*Wait, you had a crush on Taryn?* Huh. Well, what was your first memory of Bailey?" she asked, trying to get her footing.

Brogan tore his eyes away from Taryn and glanced at Bailey with a quick grin. "I can't remember really. It might have been when I came to your front door to give Taryn roses for Valentine's Day, and instead of coming down to talk to me, she sent Bailey to tell me to go find a girl my own age to give them too. I ended up giving them to Bailey."

Bailey grinned and nodded her head. "My first flowers from a boy, and they were meant for my gorgeous, older sister. Oh, the bitterness," she said, laughing at the memory.

Taryn's eyes clouded over and she looked sad, as she stared at Brogan across the table. "I'm sorry I was such a brat to you, Brogan. I'm so sorry," she said, sounding close to tears.

Brogan smiled gently across the table at her and shrugged. "I'm tough, Taryn. I don't give up."

Taryn flicked her hand toward Bailey and sniffed. "*Yeah*, Brogan. You do."

Brogan clenched his jaw lightly and sat forward. "It's been *ten* years, Taryn. How long did you expect me to wait?"

Taryn pushed her chair back from the table and without answering, walked quickly out of the room, toward the kitchen. Brogan immediately stood up and excused himself, following right behind her.

Rob cleared his throat, smiling widely and gestured to the platter of garlic bread. "Kam, could you pass the bread. Mom, this dinner is delicious. What do you think, Kam?"

Kam nodded his head quickly as he passed the bread. "Best dinner I've had in months, Anne."

Anne frowned and looked at the two vacated seats and then at Bailey, completely ignoring Rob and Kam. "Am I missing something here? Bailey, I thought *you* were dating Brogan? Why does it seem as if he's in love with Taryn?"

Rob made a coughing sound and Kam cleared his throat as Bailey stared at her plate, still filled with food. "Um, *well*, Brogan has had feelings for Taryn for a very long time. I think that maybe Taryn is a little conflicted where Brogan is concerned."

Anne glared at Bailey and sat up. "Do you mean, you're dating a man, that you *know* your sister has feelings for? Bailey! How could you? What kind of sister does something like that?" she demanded, her face turning red.

Bailey groaned and leaned her head back against her chair, as she felt Kam's hand creep back into hers. She glanced at him and for the first time he looked quite happy. "Anne, please don't blame, Bailey. She wasn't trying to hurt her sister. She had good intentions," Kam said, trying to divert Anne's wrath.

Anne glared at Bailey and sniffed loudly. "The pathway to hell is paved with good intentions, Kam. I have a headache now. I'll be in my room. Bailey, you can clean up the kitchen before you leave," she said, with a flip of her stiff hair, and walked out of the dining room.

Bailey's mouth fell open in shock, and she stared around the table at her brother, Wren and Kam. "What just happened?"

Rob laughed and took a bite of his crab cake. "You're the bad sister now. You obviously tried to steal your sister's man, and Mom will never forgive you. But on the positive side, she couldn't care less that you had a boyfriend last week named Dean. Problem solved."

Wren smiled gently at her. "Don't worry about it, Bailey. Anne will forget all about your betrayal as soon as Taryn and Brogan get together. Brogan will smooth things out with Anne for you."

Bailey nodded, but felt a little hollow inside at the horror and blame she had seen in her mother's eyes. "Holy cow, I'm the bad kid now. It was always Rob and Taryn getting into trouble and now I'm the black sheep. This is so weird."

Rob laughed, apparently delighted by the new change. He stood up and grabbed Wren's hand pulling her beside him. "Wren and I have to go. Her dad, brother and sister are coming up for a few days and they'll be at Wren's house soon. We'd like to stay and help you clean up everything, but . . . well, Mom wouldn't approve. See ya, Kam."

Rob and Wren walked out, leaving her suddenly alone with Kam. All of the drama of dinner didn't seem to be dampening Kam's appetite at all. He reached for the platter of crab cakes and helped himself to more, as she continued to shake her head in consternation.

"I have to fix this," she muttered, and pushed back her chair. She walked into the kitchen but Brogan and Taryn were nowhere in sight. She hurried to the front room and peeked out the window but Taryn's car was gone. They'd left.

She wandered back into the dining room and flopped down on her chair, feeling deflated and strange. "They're gone. Taryn and Brogan took off. Rob and Wren are gone. It's just you and me."

Kam grinned and wiped his mouth with his napkin. "Excellent. Exactly what I had planned when I agreed to come. Come on, I'll help you clean up later. Let's go sit down in the family room."

Bailey allowed herself to be pulled into the family room and sat down on the large, overstuffed leather couch. Kam sat down right next to her and put his arm around her shoulders, pulling her in close to his side. She suddenly found her head leaning back against his shoulder and pulled her knees up as she relaxed into his warmth.

"Sometimes, I feel like my life is one big Twilight Zone episode."

Kam shook his head and played with her hair, wrapping it around his finger. "Nah, this is all pretty normal. You should see my family. I'm the eldest of eight children. Trust me, you haven't seen wild."

Bailey smiled and looked up at him. "I've met Pule and your mom and dad, but I'd like to meet the rest of your family someday."

Kam nodded and smiled at her. "You will."

Bailey sighed and snuggled into Kam's side. "I guess I wasn't really thinking when I decided to bring Brogan. I just figured if we could crack through Taryn's control and get her to admit that she does have feelings for Brogan, then everything would be okay. But now, I feel like the other woman, all weird and icky. Do you think Taryn's mad at me?" she asked, in a small voice.

Kam shook his head. "From where I was sitting, I didn't sense any anger aimed at you. I think Taryn was focused on Brogan. I'm a little worried about his life right now, to be honest."

Bailey laughed and reached over and traced a line of Kam's tattoo. "I'm always so fascinated by your tattoo. Why did you get it?" she asked curiously.

Kam shrugged and slouched down on the couch, getting more comfortable. "I was young and very proud of my heritage. My family moved from Samoa when I was just a baby, but my parents were always determined that we wouldn't lose our culture. When I was at college, me and Tate and some of my Samoan buddies, went to a guy we knew from the Islands, and we all got tribal tattoos so we'd never forget who we are. Does it bother you?" he asked, looking at her closely.

Bailey looked up quickly and shook her head. "I remember the first day I met you, I saw this huge guy with long hair and a tattoo on his arm, and I remember thinking, *wow, that guy is hot,* and then I remember thinking, *too bad.*"

Kam frowned and weaved his fingers through hers. "Why, *too bad?*"

Bailey frowned, her cheeks turning pink as she looked away. "Because you're so different than me. I couldn't picture you and me together."

Kam sighed. "Because I'm Samoan and you're white? Because you're a college graduate and I'm not? Because I have tattoos and you don't?"

Bailey bit her lip and nodded. "Yeah, I guess that sounds really shallow, huh?" she asked quietly.

Kam pursed his lips and looked at the ceiling. "A little. If you want to know what I thought when I first saw you, I'd say that when you walked into the room, my heart literally flipped over in my chest. I just stared at you and thought, *wow, there she is.*"

Bailey smiled and began playing with Kam's necklace made out of black shiny stones. "There she is? What do you mean?"

Kam leaned over and kissed her lightly. "There's the woman who could break my heart."

Bailey frowned and shook her head. "But I don't want to break your heart."

Kam touched her cheek, tilting her face up so that she was looking at him. "Then don't."

Bailey blinked slowly and stared into Kam's deep, brown eyes and felt something move inside her heart. She reached up and pulled Kam's ponytail of long wavy black hair over his shoulder and touched the strands, running them through her fingers. "Kam, what are we doing?" she whispered.

Kam moved in closer so they were nose to nose. "You've decided to be brave and I've decided to love you."

Bailey felt a warmth take over her heart, and she smiled a little as she ran her hand over Kam's cheek and down his jaw. "Okay then," she said, and moved the two inches that separated them and kissed him gently. Kam sat very still as his arms pulled her closer. He allowed her to kiss him in a way that no one had ever done. She grew bolder and kissed his cheeks and then his temple and then back to his lips again, as if she were exploring new territory.

Kam grinned when she finally sat back and let out a breath he'd been holding. "Is it my turn?"

Bailey laughed and shook her head. "The way you kiss? If my mom walked in on you kissing me the way you did in Rob's office, she'd have a heart attack."

Kam grinned and leaned down and kissed her quickly but with an intensity that she would always love. "Fine, have it your way for now. Come on, I'll help you clean up the kitchen."

Bailey nodded and stood up, automatically reaching for Kam's hand as they walked into her mom's kitchen. She stared morosely at the trashed kitchen and sighed. "This is going to take forever."

Kam grimaced and stretched. "It's not The Iron Skillet, that's for sure."

A half an hour later, they had the first load of dishes loaded and washing in the dishwasher. They had all the food put away and the counters and the dining room table wiped down.

"Taryn can do the rest. Come on, let's get out of here before my mom comes out and grounds me."

Kam nodded in agreement. "It's only three o'clock. We still have the rest of the day to be together."

Bailey looked at him shyly. "That sounds really nice. I'd like that."

Kam grinned and grabbed her hand. "Let's go then."

They drove down to the beach at Point Defiance and walked along the water's edge and just talked as they held hands. When they stopped and sat down on a bench, she stared at their clasped hands resting on Kam's knee, and ran her finger over his large knuckles.

"Look at our hands, Kam. It's kind of beautiful, huh?" she asked softly, staring at their hands entwined. "Your hand is so large and dark, and mine is small and pale. You wouldn't think they'd fit together."

Kam nodded and lifted her hand and kissed the back. "But they do fit together. That's what's beautiful about you and me Bailey. In a world that would tell you that we're too different to be together, we prove that we do."

Bailey smiled and looked away from their hands and into Kam's eyes. "*Why?* Why do you like me, Kam? I mean, I know why I like you. Even though I've tried hard not to."

Kam laughed and put his arm around her shoulders bringing her in close. "Ah, Bailey, why did you have to fight it so hard?"

Bailey shrugged, blushing a little. "A few reasons I guess. But I can't seem to help it. I look at you and you're this wild, beautiful man, large and powerful, yet kind and sweet and protective too. The way you protected Wren was so amazing. I was impressed. But mad too."

Kam raised an eyebrow. "Mad?"

Bailey nodded. "I was jealous. I thought you liked Wren and that maybe you were trying to steal her away from Rob."

Kam laughed and kissed her cheek. "I protected Wren because she's my friend. I protect the people I love, Bailey."

Bailey sighed and felt a sense of rightness for once as she leaned her head on Kam's shoulder. "And me? Why out of all the girls you know, do you like me? I know we have this strange chemistry thing, but there have to be other girls you could like?

What about all of those beautiful Samoan girls, your parents probably want you to date?"

Kam sighed and nuzzled her head with his chin. "I've dated plenty of beautiful Samoan girls. And you're right, my parents would jump for joy if I fell in love with someone who shared my same heritage, but I just didn't. I tried, but it wasn't there for me, no matter how hard I tried. I like you, Bailey, because I can't seem to help it. It could be our chemistry, but it's more than that too. I look at you and everything clicks into place for me. No eyes could be more beautiful than your beautiful, blue eyes. Your hair just makes me want to run my hands through it and your face was created just for my happiness in mind. I could stare at your face all day long and never get bored."

Bailey frowned and looked away. "So, you're just attracted to what you see then?"

Kam took her chin and forced her to look at him. "That's part of it, yes, but that's not all. I'm attracted to you because of your love for your family, your loyalty and your kindness. I love your spirit and your laugh. I love how you try so hard to be good, even when underneath it, you're just a little wild. I love how when you look at me, you get this tiny little smile around your lips and your eyes go all soft and sweet. I love how when you walk in the room, I know it before I even turn around."

Bailey grinned and kissed Kam lightly. "Me too. I started thinking I have ESP or something, because I can always tell when you're nearby. I get this little shiver of electricity, this awareness when you come in the room. I didn't know you had it too. I like that," she said softly, staring up into his big, brown eyes.

Kam grinned down at her and licked his lips. "Bailey, I want you to be my girlfriend. You and me. No one else. No more dates with idiots in suits. No more looking for the perfect man. Just you and me."

Bailey's mouth fell open and she stared at Kam in surprise. She'd been so sure that Dean had wanted to be her boyfriend, but in the end, it was the last thing he'd wanted. And here was Kam, offering her commitment and stability and love so freely.

She stared at Kam's strong beautiful face and sighed a little before she nodded her head, with a small smile. "Let's try it out."

Kam laughed and tilted his head back and stared up at the sky. "Well, that was underwhelming."

Bailey winced and looked away. "I'm sorry, Kam. But like I said, there was a reason I went for Dean. He was safe and I could handle him. He didn't scare me. With you, all of my emotions are out of the boxes I've shoved them into. With you, I'm jumping out of a plane without a parachute. This is kind of terrifying for me."

Kam frowned, his eyes turning dark and sad. "*Why*, Bailey? I don't understand. Why is being with me so terrifying for you?"

Bailey looked away and let out a shaky breath. "Because it would be so easy to love you," she whispered.

Kam grabbed her and lifted her up and sat her on his lap before wrapping his large, strong arms around her. "Oh, Baby, don't be scared of loving me. I'm the one man you should never be scared of loving. I'll never let you down."

Bailey wrapped her arms around Kam's neck and hid her face in his neck as she felt her heart pounding in her chest. He ran his hand up and down her back soothingly until her breathing slowed down and she was able to lift her face and look at him.

"I've heard that before though," she said quietly.

Kam frowned darkly and looked away. "You've loved another man before?"

Bailey nodded her head slowly as the familiar sadness and shame washed over her. "Yes, I did. And it was a horrible disaster. It was the worst experience of my life. It's been seven years and I haven't seriously dated another man in all that time. I kind of feel scarred and broken most of the time."

Kam's eyes softened as he pushed her hair away from her face. "Then it's time to heal, Bailey. Let your heart love again. You're not fully alive, if you're not loving someone."

Bailey looked down at Kam's necklace and let out a long breath and nodded her head. "I want to live again. I want to love again. I'm so tired of always holding myself back, from feeling all of the emotions I have. It was dangerous before, so it's hard to trust myself."

Kam nodded and caressed her lips. "So, I'll ask again then. Bailey, would you do me the honor of being my girlfriend?"

Bailey grinned and nodded her head. "I'd love to."

Kam laughed happily and pulled her in close, nuzzling her neck. "That's more like it," he said.

Bailey laughed too and shook her head. "My poor mother. What will she think of me now? Last week Dean. Brogan this afternoon. And now you."

Kam shrugged and kissed her lightly. "Your mom loves me. She'll be so happy I stole you away from Brogan. It was pretty obvious Taryn has feelings for him. Your mom is probably right now wondering if this weird love triangle between you, Brogan and Taryn are in, is going to tear the family apart."

Bailey smiled and pulled Kam's long black ponytail over his shoulder. "Well, when you put it that way, it sounds like you're the perfect solution."

Kam stood up and set her down on her feet. "You got that right. Come on, let's go back to my house. I need to introduce my beautiful girlfriend to my mom and dad."

Bailey froze and Kam looked back at her with a raised eyebrow. "Problem?"

Bailey squinched up her face but shook her head. "No problem," she wheezed out. "I've just never done this before. Meeting the parents. I've seen the movie with Ben Stiller. These things don't usually go very well. And you did say that your parents would prefer a nice, Samoan girl. Maybe you should break it to them easy over the next week or two, and *then* invite me over?"

Kam frowned and shook his head. "Bailey, ever since I met you, I've planned on you and me being together. Trust me, this won't be a surprise."

Bailey frowned, not knowing what that meant, but followed Kam as they walked back to her car. She followed Kam's instructions and soon they were in a small subdivision in Tacoma.

"Pull into that house there," he said, pointing to an older two story home with three cars parked in front.

She followed Kam to the front door and felt incredibly nervous all of a sudden. She pulled on Kam's hand before he could open the door. "Wait! How do I look? I haven't even checked my makeup in hours. Do I look okay?" she asked nervously.

Kam rolled his eyes and grabbed her in his arms, leaning her over as he kissed her the only way he knew how to. Passionately. After a few minutes, he raised his head, his eyes bright and happy.

"You're the most beautiful woman in the world, Bailey. Now forget about your hair and that piece of spinach in your teeth and smile."

Bailey squawked and turned to run for the car, but Kam picked her up by the waist and twirled her around so she was facing the door again. "I was kidding about the spinach. Relax," he ordered.

Bailey closed her eyes and took in what she hoped was a soothing breath. "Okay. Let's do this," she said grimly, and gestured for him to open the door.

Kam grinned and opened the door for her, ushering her inside. The first thing that hit her was the noise. She could hear kids playing and laughing and yelling. Then the smells hit her. Sunday dinner, of course. Pork and other smells she couldn't put a name to. The house was decorated with lots of color and textures. On every wall were pictures of Kam's family. The journalist in her tried to take in as many details as she could.

"What do you think?" Kam asked, smiling at his home.

Bailey nodded her head and smiled up at him, putting her hand in his. "I like it. It suits you. You're going to think my apartment is very bland and boring though, compared to this."

Kam shook his head. "If you're there, I won't care. Come on. My parents are back here," he said, pulling her back to a large family room where there were so many people, she blinked in surprise.

"All of these people are your family?" she whispered. Coming from a home where she had one brother and one sister and a mom, seeing the sheer number of people packed in the family room was mind blowing.

Kam held their two hands up in the air and whistled loudly. Bailey swallowed nervously as the room went completely silent.

"I want to introduce you to my girlfriend. Everyone, this is Bailey Downing. Bailey, this is my family," he said, gesturing to the people staring at her with surprised, curious looks on their faces.

Bailey cleared her throat and looked up at Kam. Kam stared darkly at the people and lifted his chin. "I *said*, this is my girl-friend, Bailey Downing," he said, in a voice that was so commanding and strong, that Bailey's mouth dropped open. *Holy cow.*

Toa, Kam's father and Pika, Kam's mother, stood up and walked slowly toward them with polite but wary smiles on their faces. Bailey squeezed Kam's hand and stepped forward. He was going out on a limb for her. She could at least try and make a good impression.

"Hello Mr. and Mrs. Matafeo. We've met before at different events, but you probably don't remember me. I still remember the pig roast at Tate and Jane's wedding reception. I've never tasted anything so delicious in my life," she said, rambling on as Pika, Kam's mom stared at her with a slight smile on her face.

"No, we know who you are. Kam talks about you all the time. I'm not surprised that you are here. Kam is like his father. He's very determined and when he wants something, he gets it. You are welcome in my home," she said, with dignity.

Bailey smiled and glanced up at Kam. Kam grinned down at her and put his hand on her waist. "She's right. You didn't have a chance. Dad, this is Bailey. Bailey, this is my father, Toa Matafeo."

Toa bowed his head to her and smiled in a very reserved way, that had Bailey feeling nervous. "Mr. Matafeo, it's an honor to meet you. Your son is one of the best men I know. You must be an amazing father."

Toa's smile relaxed a little and his eyes brightened. "Kam is a good son. He sometimes makes decisions I don't agree with, but he is an honorable man. You are welcome in our home," he said, and gestured to the rest of the family. He pointed to each face in the room and rattled off interesting names she'd never heard of before, and which she promptly forgot. She'd have to grill Kam later so she didn't make a fool of herself at future Matafeo gatherings.

Pule, who worked as a prep cook at the Iron Skillet walked into the room with a few younger boys and grinned when he caught sight of her. "Ah, no way! I bet Antonio twenty bucks she'd never give you the time of day. *Dang*," he said, shaking his head.

Kam growled at his younger brother and moved towards him, causing Pule to jump in response. Bailey laughed and pulled back on Kam's arm. "No violence on Sunday, Kam."

Kam glared at Pule, but slipped his arm back around her waist. "Betting against your own brother, Pule? Dad, you better have a talk with him. No family loyalty at all."

Bailey laughed as Toa turned and glared at Pule. He might not be happy with Kam for bringing her home, but he wasn't happy at all with the fact that Pule doubted he could.

"Pule, in the kitchen now. Bring Kam and Bailey some dessert. Move," he ordered sternly.

Pule sighed loudly and rolled his eyes. He smiled at Bailey though and nodded his head. "You sure you want to date Kam? I could tell you stories about him that would make you run for your car. Come to the kitchen with me and I'll fill you in."

Kam jumped for Pule so quickly Bailey gasped in surprise.

Pule screamed in fear as Kam picked the teenager up in his arms, and carried him out of the room, leaving her alone with all of Kam's relatives. She smiled timidly at the people who were still staring at her warily. Pika stepped forward and took her arm. "Come sit by me, Bailey. I would like you to tell me about yourself."

Bailey nodded her head and took the seat Pika pointed out to her. She started with her childhood and losing her father at an early age. She talked very little about high school and focused on college and her career as a journalist. Toa picked up the Sunday paper and handed it to her

"Which article is yours?" he asked.

Bailey licked her lips and opened the paper to the politics section. She pointed to the article she'd written about Common Core on the front of the section, where her name was in bold letters. "That's me. I write about politics and court cases and sometimes about the educational system."

Toa took the paper back and glanced over the article and stared at her name in bold black letters. "That's good then," he said quietly, and for some reason he looked slightly happier. Pika took the paper from her husband and glanced over the article as well.

"Kam needs a smart woman to keep him on his toes. Kam talks about you often. He has liked you for a long time now. Do you care for him as much as he cares for you?" she asked so bluntly, that Bailey blinked in surprise.

She looked up, searching for some way to answer the question when Kam appeared in the doorway, grinning happily. He paused in the doorway, leaning against the wood casing and smiled at her. Bailey felt her heart warm pleasantly as she stared back at him. He radiated life and kindness and happiness. How had she resisted him for as long as she had?

Pika touched her arm and brought her back from her thoughts. "No need to answer. I just saw it on your face. You love my son. It is good then."

Bailey's eyes widened in shock and she looked down at her hands, at a complete loss as how to respond to that.

"Did you just embarrass my girlfriend, mom? Why is she blushing like that?" Kam asked dryly, now standing right in front of her.

Pika smiled placidly and made a waving motion with her hands. "I wanted to know if she cared for you as much as you cared for her, and I saw her face when you walked in the room. It's obvious to anyone with eyes, isn't it? You two will be good. This is a good match."

Kam's eyes lit up as he grinned down at her. Bailey bit her lip and looked away in embarrassment. She had agreed to be Kam's girlfriend just an hour ago and already his mom had announced to the entire room that she was in love with Kam. *Just great.*

"I'm going to show Bailey the backyard. Pule had to change clothes so he can bring us some dessert when we come back in," he said, pulling Bailey up to stand next to him.

Bailey smiled at everyone as Kam pulled her through the room, to the sliding glass doors leading to the back yard. As soon as the doors shut behind her, she let out a breath and felt her shoulder sag in relief. "Wow, I didn't think I'd survive," she muttered, pulling her hand through her long hair.

Kam laughed and pulled her to a large hammock, hanging between two trees. Kam sat on the middle and pulled her down next to him. He smoothly twisted both of their bodies so that within a few seconds they were both lying in the hammock, staring up at the white blossoms in the tree branches above them.

"You did great, Bailey. My parents love you."

Bailey snorted and turned her body so she could put an arm around Kam's large chest as she rested her head on his shoulder. "Your parents are stoically resigned to the idea of me. That's slightly different than loving me."

Kam grunted and kissed her forehead. "I saw my mom's face. She's good. My dad always takes a while to warm up to people.

You should have seen them with Jane. She had it kind of rough. They disowned Tate for a while and it was horrible. They don't want to go through that again, so they've learned to be accepting of their children's choices."

Bailey winced and made a note to talk to Jane about her experiences with Toa and Pika. "Would you choose to be disowned, to be with me?"

Kam looked down at her and his eyes softened. "As if you have to ask. I'd face down anybody and everything for you, Bailey."

Bailey smiled and sighed happily, as she rested her head against his shoulder again. "Are you real?"

Kam chuckled. "So real, all other men will fade from your memory. All that will be left, is you and me."

Bailey frowned and closed her eyes. "I hope so," she said softly.

They spent the next hour in the hammock, talking and laughing, until Pule called for them to come in and get their dessert. She almost upended the hammock trying to get out and Kam laughed, before plucking her out of the hammock and carrying her to the back door, kissing her quickly before opening the door for her.

Bailey walked in with red cheeks and bright eyes. Kam joined her and automatically put a protective arm around her shoulder. Conversation picked up again and Kam led her to a table, where two large pieces of chocolate cake waited for them.

"Oh, I was expecting a Samoan dessert. This looks pretty basic," she said, sitting down and picking up her fork.

Kam nodded and took a big bite. "We do eat a lot of traditional Samoan food, but we're pretty mainstream American too. We eat tacos and hamburgers and pot roast. We're more alike than we're different."

Bailey nodded her head and glanced back at all of the people still looking at her and quickly turned back to her cake. "Do you think they'll get used to me at some point?"

Kam glanced back over his shoulder at all of his relatives and narrowed his eyes at them. "Of course. They barely notice Jane now, when she comes over. It's no big deal, Bailey. Really, they're just curious about you."

Bailey smiled and nodded her head. She finished her cake quickly and glanced at her watch. "Well, I better get home, Kam."

Kam nodded and picked up both of their plates. He handed them to Pule with a grin and then waved his hand at his family. "I'm heading over to Bailey's house now. See you later," he said, and pulled her toward the front door.

Bailey bit her lip as she unlocked her car. "Sorry, I just felt an ulcer starting to form. I do like your family, Kam, it's just hard for me to be stared at."

Kam shrugged and buckled his seatbelt. "No worries. Like I said, they'll get used to you. You'll feel more comfortable when Tate and Jane are here. I think Jane's sister Kit had a family dinner at her house today, otherwise they would have been here. It'll just take some time."

Bailey sighed and headed out of the subdivision. "Okay."

Kam glanced at her and lifted an eyebrow. "I'm worth it, right?"

Bailey laughed, relaxing all the way and nodded her head. "Absolutely."

They spent the rest of the day relaxing at her apartment and watching movies. She made Kam a mushroom and red pepper omelet for a snack, and they talked about their experiences at college. They figured out that they were both students at WSU at the same time and Bailey had to grab all of her old yearbooks.

"Oh, my word, there you are!" she said, pointing to picture of the football team. "No wonder I never met you. You were probably dating all of the cheerleaders and partying."

Kam frowned and shook his head. "Not really. It's a lot of hard work to keep your grades up on top of all of the practices and games. Trust me, I didn't spend a lot of time dating or party-ing. What about you? Did you date much? Party much?"

Bailey frowned and shook her head. "No, for the first few years I was pretty quiet. I worked so hard, I made the Dean's list. I dated more after I graduated. I could have bumped into you at the library."

Kam frowned and sat back, closing the yearbook. "What happened, Bailey? What happened that was so bad, that you spent your college years glued to your books, instead of having fun with your friends?"

Bailey looked away and crossed her arms over her chest, feeling sad and vulnerable. "I'd really rather not talk about it," she said quietly. "This is our first day together, I'd rather spend it being happy with you, instead of talking about the past."

Kam sighed but nodded his head. "Fine. But someday soon, I want you to trust me enough to tell me what broke your heart."

Bailey nodded her head but looked away quickly. "Okay. Soon."

When she drove Kam home later and kissed him goodbye, she watched him walk away and wondered if he'd look at her the same way, if he knew her past. She didn't want to bet on the answer.

Chapter Twelve

BLINDSIDED

Bailey went to work Monday morning, the same as usual, and wondered why everything felt so different. She was smiling at everyone, and not just some crummy, *hey, our eyes met accidently, so I'll barely lift the sides of my mouth, kind of smile.* She was smiling. She'd even worn her cutest plaid skirt and white cashmere sweater. For no reason. She'd straightened her blond streaked hair and pulled it high in a cute ponytail. And, the biggest thing of all, she left off her ugly, thick, black glasses she wore, to make sure people took her seriously. Oh, people were going to take her seriously, whether she looked good or not.

She caught a few surprised looks from her colleagues and laughed a little. It was like they weren't used to her being happy or something. She breezed into her editor's office and sat down with a grin, as she crossed her legs and smoothed her skirt over her knees.

Jackson Akers raised an eyebrow and scratched the top of his shiny, bald head. "What in the world happened to you? You look like you discovered the fountain of youth at Disneyland and won ten thousand dollars in Vegas, on your way home."

Bailey shrugged nonchalantly and studied her nails. "I had a good weekend. Try it sometime. It does wonders."

Jackson snorted and pushed his glasses up his nose, as he glance down his laptop. "I want you to head over to the court-room today. Avery Brown is up for parole, and every mother in a fifty mile radius will be there picketing, to make sure he doesn't get it. I want some interviews and an overview of the original case. We've had so many teachers in the news lately abusing students, but this one was the granddaddy of them all. Have something on my desk by three today."

Bailey swallowed sickly and stood up on shaky legs. "Of course, Jackson. Whatever you say," she said weakly, and practi-cally ran out of the office. She hurried down the hallway, ignoring everyone she'd just smiled at, and pushed her way into the women's restroom, locking herself in a stall, as she concentrated on not hyperventilating.

Fifteen minutes later, after holding cold wet paper towels to her face, she made her way to her cubicle. She kept her face down and tried not to make eye contact with anyone. She went through the motions of checking her emails, and as quickly as she could, she grabbed her laptop and escaped. She practically ran down the stairs to her car, and sat in the parking lot shud-dering uncontrollably, until she was able to fit her key into the ignition.

She wanted desperately to go home and crawl under her covers, and not come out for weeks. She wanted to go to Belin-da's Bakery and order the biggest chocolate cupcake they made. She wanted to run to The Iron Skillet, and find her brother and ask him to make everything better again. She wanted to find Kam. If she could just feel Kam's strong, powerful arms around her, she'd be okay.

She drove to her favorite spot, overlooking the Puget Sound and got out of her car. She collapsed on the newly green grass and burst into tears. She wiped the scalding hot tears off her cheeks and wondered how in the world, she could go to the courtroom and interview all the moms there, upset that a sexual predator could possibly be set free.

She lifted her face to the cloudy sky above her and prayed for strength. And then she prayed that no one would ever find out that her first boyfriend had been Avery Brown . . . *her softball coach and history teacher.*

Chapter Thirteen

TROUBLE AHEAD

Kam had Monday off from The Iron Skillet, so he spent it running errands, helping his mom fix the bathroom light, and hanging out with Tate, his cousin who was more of a brother than his actual brothers. Tate met him at the new Thai restaurant in Tacoma by the Tacoma Dome.

He walked in and Tate waved him over to a table by the window. Tate always ordered peanut pad Thai, but he was in the mood for a spicy curry. He told the waitress his order and waited for Tate to hem and haw, before ordering his usual.

"How's Jane doing?" Kam asked, picking up a pot sticker Tate had ordered for them.

Tate grinned and sat back in his chair, resting his head in his hands. "Jane's amazing. Jane is beautiful. Jane is perfect," he said, closing his eyes and smiling contentedly.

Kam laughed and popped another pot sticker in his mouth. "A man in love, is a beautiful thing. Kind of silly to look at, but still beautiful."

Tate laughed and grabbed the last pot sticker. "Interesting you should bring up love. I got an interesting call from Mom last night. Seems like she's worried about you. She said something about you being in love with a sharp, little blond who was too beautiful for her own good. Said something about the way you looked at her. *What was it?*" Tate paused, with a delighted grin. "Oh yeah, she said Kam is so in love, he couldn't see straight."

Kam cleared his throat and took a sip of water. "Mom did not say that."

Tate laughed. "You're right, that was Dad. Mom said she liked her, but she was worried you'd get your heart broken."

Kam grimaced and sat back in his chair. "You know what Mom and Dad are like. Look how worried they were about you."

Tate nodded his head, his brown eyes gleaming at his cousin. "Oh, I remember. It's hard to forget being disowned, over the woman you love."

Kam sighed but perked up as their waitress brought over their entrees. "Oh man, this looks good," he muttered, before digging in.

Tate followed suit and they were silent for a few minutes before resuming their conversation. "Bailey Downing?"

Kam looked up with a frown. "Yeah, how'd you know? Did Mom tell you?"

Tate shook his head. "She didn't have to. Everyone who has seen you around Bailey knows you're head over heels. Saturday, at the rugby game, you ran right to her. I believe you had your arm around her? Possibly eating a cupcake out of her hand? Sound familiar?"

Kam reddened and shrugged. "Maybe so. And yes, it's Bailey. I've liked her for a while now. I asked her to be my girlfriend yesterday, and she said yes."

Tate's eyebrows shot up and he leaned forward. "Seriously? You actually said the words, *will you be my girlfriend,* and she actually said yes?"

Kam glared at his cousin. "I'm an old fashioned kind of guy. She needs to know she can't be dating those idiots in suits anymore. We're committed to each other."

Tate nodded his head and took another bite of his noodles.

"*Hmm,* so me telling you that Meredith is coming back to town next week, won't have any effect on you at all?"

Kam groaned and looked away. "Meredith is coming back? She told me she wanted a clean start down in California."

Tate rolled his eyes. "She called Jane last night and told her she was too homesick. She wants to start over here. With a new job and um, with *you* too."

Kam's eyes went wide in surprise and he put his fork down. "That's not good."

Tate laughed. "No, Kam, it is not good. You know how, *in your face,* and crazy Meredith can be. She told Jane, she had realized too late that she was actually in love with you. She says she'll do anything to get you back. The question is, do you want her to? You just barely started things with Bailey. Do you still have feelings for Meredith?"

Kam sighed and twirled his noodles around his fork. "I really liked Meredith. She was fun to be around. I cared about her a lot. But it's completely different from the way I feel about Bailey. There's no comparison, Tate. Bailey takes my breath away. I look at her and my heart just melts. I love her, man."

Tate paused, and lowered his fork back to his plate as he frowned at his cousin. "You're serious."

Kam nodded his head firmly. "Deadly. The first time I saw Bailey, it was like a truck hit me in the chest. She's everything, Tate. I would do anything for her."

Tate nodded his head and smiled. "Sounds just like how I felt with Jane. I'll have Jane give Meredith a head's up, so she doesn't mess things up between you and Bailey when she gets back in town."

Kam smiled in relief. "Thanks, man, I appreciate it."

Tate signaled the waitress and ordered another plate of pot stickers. "So, are you seeing her tonight? It's your day off. Any romantic plans with the woman you love?"

Kam smiled and shrugged. "It's my day off, but not hers. She's a reporter for the News Tribune. And she's an incredible writer. I've read almost all of her articles. She's so sharp. She gets down to the essence of the problem with the precision of a surgeon. She's brilliant, Tate. Our children are going to be smart and gorgeous."

Tate laughed, his shoulders shaking. "Oh, Kam, you're in so much trouble. Falling in love with a woman like that is dangerous."

Kam rolled his eyes. "I can handle Bailey. You know why? Because she might not realize it yet, but she loves me, just as much I love her. She's just scared for some reason."

Tate frowned and nodded. "Move slow then, Kam. Don't go so fast, that she runs away."

Kam shook his head. "I can't. Every time I see her, I have to stop myself from throwing myself on my knees and begging her to marry me."

Tate winced and took a sip of water. "Kam, I love you like you were my brother, so I'm only telling you this for your own good. Take your time. She's a sweet girl, smart and beautiful but the impression she gave me, was that she was very skittish around men."

Kam shrugged. "Not me though. She trusts me, Tate and like I said, I think she loves me."

Tate nodded his head. "Which means, you're even more terrifying. Just go slow."

Kam took out his wallet and threw down some bills before standing up. "Not in my vocabulary, bro. Give Jane a kiss from me," he said, and walked out.

Kam stepped out into the pale sunlight and sighed. Tate was an idiot. He didn't know Bailey, like he did. Bailey just needed the right man in her life. And that was him.

Chapter Fourteen
BAILEY'S SECRET

Bailey began interviewing the women holding signs outside the courthouse, and felt a cold numbness encase her. As she listened to story after story, of ruined lives and of women who were still broken, because of one man, she felt something she'd been hanging onto for six years crack open inside of her. The last woman she interviewed was a few years older than her. Dark haired, thin and attractive. She was holding the hand of a small child and holding a sign that read, *He Destroyed My Life. He'll Do It Again.* She asked the woman to tell her story and stood there, frozen as the woman described the exact same thing that had happened to her, all those years ago. The special attention. The extra credit and good grades. The phone calls. The presents. The kissing. The sexual relationship.

If this woman, this victim, was brave enough to stand in front of the world and hold up a sign, telling her truth, *why couldn't she even tell one person?* She felt like reaching out and touching the woman's arm and saying, *I know. It happened to me too.* But her mouth didn't move and the moment was gone. As she walked slowly away from the women, it felt like there was a living, breathing, whirlwind inside of her and she didn't know how to push it down anymore. She didn't know if it was possible.

She drove home after taking pictures of the angry women holding signs and walked inside her apartment and over to her desk. She set her laptop down and opened it up, sitting down in front of her computer and staring at the blank document, just waiting to be filled with words. *Her words.*

She held her fingers out toward the keys and let them fall. *Finally*, she let them fall and her words started pouring out. Her story, her life, her anguish and her shame poured out of her as if she'd been cut open. Line after line after line, she wrote until she couldn't write any more. She scanned through it for errors and then emailed it to her editor before she could change her mind. This one, she wouldn't be handing in, in person. She couldn't.

She stood up and covered her mouth with her hands before collapsing on her knees and letting the tears from six years ago, finally wash her clean.

It was over.

She lay there on her floor, in front of her desk for what seemed like an hour, before she finally pulled herself up and turned on the shower. She stripped down and stood under the hot, soothing water, for as long as she could, before drying off and laying on her bed, hollowed out, and empty.

The sound of her phone had her searching for her cell. On the sixth ring she picked up. "Are you sure, Bailey?"

Bailey let out a sigh that might have been a sob and nodded her head. "Yes, Jackson. I'm sure."

He was silent for a very long time before answering. "You're a strong woman, Bailey. Take tomorrow off. There'll be a big reaction to this."

Bailey swallowed. "I know," she said softly, and hung up. There were only a few reactions she was worried about though. Her mom. Taryn. Rob. And Kam.

She turned over on her stomach and jerked in response to her ringtone. She glanced at her cell and blinked sadly. *Kam.* She laid the phone down on her bed and turned her head away from it. She couldn't talk to him. Not until he knew. Not until he realized who he'd fallen for.

Chapter Fifteen

MELTDOWN

Kam walked into work the next day feeling grim and worried. Bailey hadn't answered her phone even once the day before, and he'd left countless texts. At 11pm, she'd finally responded with one text. *Read the paper tomorrow.*

That was it. Sunday they'd accepted their feelings for one another. He'd introduced her to his family and the very next day, she shut him out. Tate might have been right. Maybe taking it slow with Bailey was the route to go. Maybe it was the only route available. He glared at the floor before tying on his apron. Was it worth it? Was Bailey worth all this angst and self-doubt? He closed his eyes and thought of the woman he loved and sighed. *Yes.*

Wren pushed through the kitchen door, all smiles and full of energy. He smiled at her and waved at Cynthia and Antonio. Pule walked in five minutes late and Kam glared at him. Pule needed a kick in the rear, if he thought he could slack around at The Iron Skillet. He opened his mouth to say so, when Rob walked through the door. He looked upset and unhappy. Wren walked quickly to him and put her hand on his arm. Rob leaned down and kissed her cheek but shook his head. He scanned the kitchen until his eyes fell on him.

"Kam, can I see you please?"

Kam frowned but nodded his head. Wren looked at him questioningly but he had no idea why Rob would want to see him privately. Unless, it was about Bailey. Kam scowled. If Bailey had changed her mind about being with him and had asked her older brother to break up with him for her, he was going to lose it. He stomped into Rob's office and shut the door. Probably more loudly than he should have.

Rob didn't seem to notice though. His hair was already a spiky mess, as if he'd run his hands through his hair over and over. "Kam, have a seat."

Kam sat down, feeling even more murderous. *Have a seat?* Bailey was not getting away with this. No way was he going to let her run away from her feelings for him. She'd been doing that ever since they'd met and he was done.

"If this is about Bailey, Rob, don't even start, man. I love your sister. I love her and she knows how I feel about her. I don't care if you don't like it, I don't care if your mom doesn't like it. I don't care if the whole world doesn't like it. I love your sister and I'm going to date her. If you think you can sit there and tell me to back off, well you're insane. Because I'm not going to. Not now, not ever. So, just save your breath," he said, glaring at Rob, his eyes hot and mean.

Rob looked at him in surprise as he talked on and on, but then smiled a little. Rob lifted a hand and waved it in the air. "Kam, I love you. Stop being ridiculous. If you only knew how many times I tried to get you and Bailey together you'd realize how dumb you just sounded. Nah, this isn't about you, Kam. But this is about Bailey," he said, sounding so grim and upset that Kam sat up in his chair.

"What is it, Rob? Is she okay? I tried calling her all day yesterday and she wouldn't talk to me. What's happened?" he demanded, feeling a chill of foreboding.

Rob closed his eyes and let out a long, pained breath. "This is what happened yesterday," he said, and picked up the newspaper off the desk and tossed it to Kam. Kam picked it up and glanced through it, raising his eyebrows quizzically.

Rob pointed to the paper. "Second page. Editorials."

Kam flipped the paper open and immediately saw the picture of Bailey, next to the title, *What it feels like to fall in love with your teacher.* Kam felt his heart fall to his stomach, as he read the article detailing the way Avery Brown had groomed Bailey for over a year, starting when she was fifteen. She was blunt about what happened and her feelings as she documented the way a predator hunts his prey. He reached the end of the article and felt sick to his stomach. Sick and hurt and desperate to find Bailey.

"Where is she? I have to find her," he said, throwing the paper down and standing up.

Rob pinched the bridge of his nose and shook his head. "I've been calling her all morning. I've been over to her apartment, but she's not there. I talked to her editor and he told me he gave her the day off. My mom is about to have a nervous breakdown and Taryn says she can't work today. I need to find my sister, Kam. I need to find her now," he ground out.

Kam nodded his head. "I respectfully request some time off for personal reasons."

Rob looked up at him and smiled. "You're still on the clock. Find my sister, Kam. And make sure . . . make sure she's okay," he said, clearing his throat as his voice thickened dangerously.

Kam nodded his head and walked out of the office. He walked quickly back to the kitchen, whipping his apron off. He walked over to Wren who was discussing the day's menu with Cynthia and pulled her gently aside.

"Sorry, Wren, but I have to leave. I have to go find Bailey. After you're done here, go talk to Rob. He needs you."

Wren looked shocked but nodded her head. "You're leaving."

Kam nodded and grabbed his keys. "I have to find her, Wren. I'll be back when I can. Maybe," he said, and hurried out the back door. He first drove over to the bakery and found Jane but

she hadn't heard from Bailey in days. He called Tate and asked
him to keep an eye out for her car. Tate had read the paper and
agreed immediately, not even asking any questions.

He drove over to her apartment and pounded on the door for
ten minutes before finding the manager and convincing him to
open the door and check for her. She wasn't there though. The
apartment was completely empty. He got in his Suburban and
drove around town looking for her. He even went by Anne's
house, but she hadn't seen her. He felt horrible as he saw the tear
tracks through her makeup, attesting to the pain she was feeling
on behalf of her daughter. She begged Kam to find her too.

Kam sat in his Suburban and pounded the steering wheel.
"Where are you, Bailey?" he yelled, starting his car and driving
aimlessly down the road. On a hunch, he drove down to the
beach, where he'd asked her to be his girlfriend. He parked his
huge Suburban and ran down to the shore. He scanned the rocky
beach and sighed in disappointment. Nothing. No one.

He turned to go back to his car and noticed a small figure
huddled by a grouping of rocks. *Bailey*. He walked slowly toward
the figure, as if any sudden movements would scare her. He
walked silently toward the figure and noticed she'd wrapped an
old plaid, game blanket around her shoulders. Her head was
bowed, resting in her hands as she sat completely still and quiet.
He sat down next to her and waited until she became aware of
his presence. The sound of the ocean didn't need to be interrupted by him.

A few moments later, Bailey slowly lifted her head and looked
at him in confusion. "*Kam?*"

Kam smiled gently at her and touched her knee. "Hey, Baby.
What are you doing out here all alone? I've been worried about
you."

Bailey looked away from him, her eyes suddenly shuttered
and dark. "I just need to be alone, Kam."

Kam shook his head. "No, Bailey, you've been alone for too
long. You've held yourself apart, because of what happened to

you. Now that you've told the world what's happened, there's nothing left to fear. Come here, Bailey," he said, holding his arms open wide.

Bailey looked at him timidly from underneath the fall of her hair and shook her head. "Why would you want to hold me, Kam? You don't want to be with me. Not really. Not now," she whispered.

Kam stared at her in shock and ignored her signals to back off and scooped her up, holding her tightly in his arms, as he rocked her back and forth. "Baby, don't be silly. I love you. Just because that monster hurt you and took advantage of you, doesn't mean you're not worthy of love. You're so loved, Bailey. By your family and your friends and me."

Bailey began to weep softly. Kam let out a sigh as he felt her hand creep around his neck and she began to hold him back. He continued to hold her, rocking her back and forth as her body shook. A half an hour later, she lay exhausted against his chest.

"You came looking for me?"

Kam nodded his head, kissing her hair. "Of course, I did. If I was hurting and alone, wouldn't you come looking for me?"

Bailey nodded her head immediately. "So everyone knows then," she said.

Kam nodded his head and pushed her hair out of her face, so he could see her eyes. "Your family knows. Rob is the one who showed me the article. He's very worried about you. He was practically in tears, he's so worried. Taryn couldn't come in to work today, and I stopped by and saw your mom. She doesn't have much make-up left at this point. Your family needs you, Bailey. They're hurting for you."

Bailey nodded her head. "I knew they would. That's why I never told them. That's why I never told anyone, because I knew it would hurt my family. But yesterday, my editor told me to cover the parole hearing for Avery Brown. I went to the court-house and there were dozens of women holding signs, demanding that parole be withheld. I interviewed some of the women there, Kam and there was one woman there who looked a lot like me. Her story was identical to mine. And there she was, holding her child's hand, and holding her sign in the air for the world to see. All in the hopes that it might protect someone else. And there I was, completely silent about what he'd done to me. I couldn't be silent anymore, Kam. I can't be silent ever again."

Kam nodded his head and kissed her cheek. "What stopped it, Bailey?"

Bailey sighed tiredly and leaned back against his chest. "I thought I was the only one. I thought he loved me. But at the end of my junior year, a girl came forward and reported him. And then, another girl came forward and another. One of the girls was pregnant. So many girls came forward, that I felt like maybe I didn't have to. That's why he's in jail, because of those brave girls. I was a coward, Kam. I was too embarrassed and ashamed to tell everyone what had happened. I was too weak."

Kam frowned and shook his head. "Bailey, you were a young girl. You were scared and horrified. No one is judging you. No one. Besides, you kind of made up for it with that article. There's no way Avery is making parole now."

Bailey nodded her head and ran her hands up and down his t-shirt. "I don't want this affecting my life anymore, Kam. He's kept me in the dark for so long. I just want to be in the light. With you."

Kam nodded his head and covered her hand with his over his heart. "Then it's time to come out into the light. I know an amazing therapist if you're interested. She worked with Tate when he was a teenager. It might help to talk to somebody about what happened to you."

Bailey licked her lips and looked up into his eyes. "I think that's probably a good idea. Do you . . . do you still want to be with me, now that you know?"

Kam smiled and nodded his head. "I do, Bailey. I want to be with you forever. Just because someone hurt you, in no way makes you any less beautiful, any less kind or any less amazing."

Bailey blinked a few times and then smiled shyly. "People are going to look at me differently now."

Kam nodded his head. "Maybe, but does that matter? Your friends will look at you now, and see a strong woman who survived something horrible. They'll love you even more. Strangers might look at you differently, and they'll see the same thing. You're going to be fine, Bailey. I promise. And I'll be right there with you. I won't let anyone hurt you ever again."

Bailey reached up and touched Kam's cheek with her thumb. "How did I get so lucky finding you?"

Kam grinned, feeling his heart start to beat again. "You got it wrong. How did I get so lucky finding you?"

Bailey laughed lightly and then leaned forward and kissed him softly on the lips. "I love you, Kam," she whispered, as she closed her eyes and wrapped her arms around his neck tightly.

Kam felt his heart expand so much that it felt like his whole body was filled with light. "I love you too. Now let's get you back to the restaurant. I'm going to make you a big bowl of truffle cream, Mac and Cheese, and you're going to tell your big brother you're okay. You know how much he loves you and this is eating him up."

Bailey nodded her head. "I know you have to work today, but I don't want to be alone."

Kam kissed her head and stood up with her in his arms. He began to walk back to his Suburban and opened the door for her, setting her down in the seat. He leaned in the doorway as she looked up at him, her eyes pleading with him. "I'm not working today, Bailey. I'm taking a personal day to spend with my girlfriend. She had a rotten day and she needs me. And that's okay. Because it's good to need people."

Bailey sighed and closed her eyes with a small smile on her mouth. "I think I can actually get through this, if you're by my side."

Kam leaned forward and kissed her cheek. "You've already made it through, Bailey."

Kam drove her back to the restaurant and walked her back to Rob's office. He stood with her in the doorway, as Rob finally looked up from his desk and saw his sister. His face lit up and he jumped up and ran around his desk, picking Bailey up in his arms and holding her tightly.

Kam noticed a few tears on Rob's face and felt a little choked up himself. Rob set her down on the floor and cupped her face in his hands. "I'm going to kill him. And then I'm going to kill you, for not telling me, so I could kill him. *Ah,* Bailey, why didn't you tell us?" Rob asked, hugging her again.

Bailey wiped her eyes and looked back at him helplessly. Kam reached out and grabbed Bailey's hand and pushed them both into Rob's office, so he could shut the door. "Rob, Bailey knew it would hurt you. She was trying to protect you."

Rob stared at him like he was insane. "It's not her job to protect me. It's *my* job to protect *her. It's my job,"* he said, his fists clenched at his side.

Bailey sighed and nodded her head. "I love you, Rob. Please forgive me."

Rob stared at his sister and shook his head. He turned around so he and Bailey couldn't see his face, but Kam could hear Rob weeping. Bailey stood up slowly and walked around to face her brother. "*Rob?*"

Rob shook his head. "Don't you ever ask for forgiveness for this. Don't you ever ask for forgiveness. This was not your fault. He was a predator and you were so young, Bailey. Don't you ever blame yourself," Rob said, wiping his eyes.

Bailey leaned down and hugged Rob, just as the office door burst open. Bailey looked up in surprise, to see Taryn in the doorway, breathing hard and red in the face. As soon as she saw Bailey, she burst into loud, horrible wrenching sobs.

Bailey groaned and looked at him. Kam did the only thing he could do. He hugged Taryn and patted her back, until she could calm down. Bailey walked timidly up to her older sister and touched her shoulder.

"Taryn, I'm so sorry," she whispered

Taryn's head whipped up and she glared at Bailey. "How can you say that to me?" she demanded, and turned back to Kam's shoulder, crying louder now.

Rob sighed and wiped his eyes before standing up and taking Taryn from Kam. "Bailey, just a thought, but maybe stop apologizing for something you shouldn't be apologizing for. It's kind of killing us."

Bailey's eyes looked confused and troubled. "Kam?"

Kam grabbed her hand and pulled her into his side. "Rob, Taryn, Bailey needs something to eat. I'm going to get her some Macaroni and Cheese. When you guys are okay, come sit with us."

Kam pulled Bailey out of the office and shut the door firmly. He walked into the dining room and grabbed Brogan. "Please seat Bailey in the back for privacy. I'm going to get her something to eat. Don't let anyone near her, okay?"

Brogan's quiet, sad eyes told him he was fully aware of the situation as he nodded his head. "Of course. Come with me, sweetheart. I'll take care of you," he said gently, and led her away.

Kam hurried to the kitchen and with terse greetings to everyone, he scooped up two bowls of noodles. Wren came to his side and grabbed his arm before he could walk out.

"Is she okay?"

Kam paused, wondering how to answer that question. "Not really, no. But she's on her way to being okay, if that makes sense. She just needs to get through today and see that life can be normal and good again. She needs to know that her family loves and supports her no matter what. Rob and Taryn are so upset right now, it's not helping much."

Wren nodded and took off her apron. "I'll go talk to them. Thanks, Kam. What would we do without you?" she asked, and leaned up and kissed him on the cheek.

Kam smiled and hurried back to Bailey. Brogan had gotten

her a glass of grape juice and was sitting next to her, holding her hand and touching her shoulder. Kam frowned a little at that, but knew Brogan was being a good friend.

"Here you go, Bailey, the best comfort food in the Pacific Northwest."

Bailey smiled up at him gratefully and took a big bite, closing her eyes in pleasure. "This is exactly what I needed," she said, with a little smile. "I don't think I've eaten anything in over a day."

Kam winced at that, wishing he could have been there for her yesterday. Brogan stood up and pounded Kam on the back. "Take good care of her, Kam," he said, and walked away.

They ate their lunch together in silence for a while, before Bailey pushed her bowl away. "I think I'm going to go home and take a nap, and then I'm going to call the therapist, make an appointment and then, you know what? I think I might just get on with my life," she said wonderingly.

Kam grinned and shook his head. "Ah, Baby, I wish you could. Sweetie, you gotta talk to your mom, before you do anything else. She's so upset, she's making herself ill. She still doesn't even know that I found you."

Bailey's face fell and she hugged her arms. "Kam, I can't do it. I can't face my mom knowing that she knows. I can't."

Kam frowned and grabbed Bailey's hand. "You can, because I'll be there with you."

Bailey shuddered and looked away. "Do I have to?"

Kam nodded his head slowly. "I'm afraid so. She loves you, Bailey. Just let her know that you're okay. That's all she needs to hear."

Bailey bit her lip and looked away. "Will you come back afterwards with me? You won't leave me today, right? You said you wouldn't."

Kam smiled and nodded his head. "I promised. I would never break a promise to you."

Bailey let out a shaky breath and nodded. "Okay then."

Rob and Taryn walked up just then and Bailey looked at them with haunted eyes. Rob grabbed a chair and pulled it over to sit next to her. He reached over and touched a strand of hair and sighed. "Sorry, I guess I'm not handling this very well, but I want you to know that I love you. And I'm so sorry you had to go through this. I'm here for you. Anything you need, I'm here for you. I just want you to know that."

Bailey smiled tremulously and nodded. "Thanks, Rob. You really are the best brother, a girl could ever have."

Rob winced but nodded his head and motioned for Taryn. Taryn pulled a chair over too and sat down, just staring at Bailey. "You're my little sister. I was supposed to look out for you. I knew something was wrong. I knew you were hiding something from me. I knew you were upset and anxious, and I was so caught up in my own stupid, little life that I never bothered to find out why. Bailey, I hope you forgive me for being the worst sister you could ever have," she said, sniffing back tears and grabbing a napkin off the table to wipe her nose.

Kam watched as Bailey reached over and pulled Taryn into her arms, comforting her and talking softly into her ear. Taryn shook her head and began to cry louder, but Bailey kept patting her back and talking. Rob wiped his eyes and motioned for someone. Brogan walked over and took one look at Taryn and covered his mouth with his hand.

"Brogan, could you take Taryn back to her office and get her an aspirin and a drink? She's not feeling very well today," Rob said quietly.

Brogan nodded and reached for Taryn's hand, pulling her up. She leaned heavily against Brogan's arm and he wrapped his arm around her, supporting her as they walked out of the dining room.

Rob sighed and stood up, leaning over to kiss Bailey on the cheek. "I'm going to go call mom and tell her what happened and that you're here and you're okay. But she'll want to talk to you herself at some point."

Bailey nodded her head. "I know. Thanks, Rob."

Rob flinched but nodded his head and patted Kam on the shoulder before walking away.

Kam watched Rob for a moment before looking back at Bailey. "You know, I might have five times the amount of relatives that you do, but the ones you have are pretty great. You have an amazing family."

Bailey nodded and smiled. "I guess I do. I think I'll give Rob some time to talk to Mom, before we head over."

Kam nodded. "That gives us just enough time to drive over to Belinda's Bakery, so I can buy you a Matafeo cupcake."

Bailey grinned and reached for his hand. "With you and that cupcake, I can face anything. Even my mother."

Kam stood up and moved so he could sit next to her and put his arm around her shoulders. "You're going to be just fine."

Bailey leaned her head against Kam's chest and closed her eyes with a sigh. "I am."

Chapter Sixteen

GIRL TROUBLES

Meredith walked up to the Iron Skillet, where Tawni had mentioned Kam was working now. She'd only eaten there a few times before. She looked at the traditional wood and rock exterior and sighed. She'd come home from California because she was homesick, but she was already missing L.A. She opened the large heavy door and walked into the dim, quiet interior and nodded her head to the blond hostess.

"No table thanks. I'm just here to see my boyfriend."

The hostess raised an eyebrow curiously and smiled. "Oh, sure. Who is your boyfriend and I'll go grab him for you."

Meredith smiled proudly, thinking of Kam Matafeo. It had been over six months since they'd seen each other and she was dying to see his beautiful face. "Kam Matafeo. I was told he's a cook here. I'll just poke my head in the kitchen, if you don't mind. I want to surprise him," she said, with a playful grin on her face.

The hostess's smile froze on her face, and she stared at Meredith as if she hadn't heard right. "Wait, did you say *Kam?*"

Meredith nodded her head and walked around the girl. *Seriously, how many guys were named Kam?* "Yeah, thanks," she said breezily, and walked down the hallway past the dining room and back to the kitchen. She pushed the door open and slipped inside and glanced around the busy kitchen, for the biggest, baddest Samoan she'd ever known.

A petite looking woman, who had her strawberry blond hair, scraped back from her face in a bun, walked up to her with a frown on her face. "Can I help you?"

Meredith frowned back before turning to stare at her surroundings. "Yeah, I'm looking for Kam Matafeo."

The woman raised an eyebrow. "He's out today. Would you like me to pass along a message to him?"

Meredith looked the woman up and down and smirked. She'd probably fallen hard for Kam. *Who wouldn't?* Well, it was going to be a huge disappointment then to know that Kam was already taken.

"Yeah, tell Kam his girlfriend came by to see him. Tell him I've missed him, but I'm back and I can't wait to jump into his arms."

The woman blinked slowly at her and shook her head. "Sweetie, are you feeling okay? You're not delusional or anything, are you?"

Meredith's mouth dropped open and she rested a hand on her hip. "Oh, no you didn't."

The woman smiled grimly back at her and gestured to the door. "Fraid so. I'll let Kam know *a friend* dropped by. What's your name so I can pass on the message?"

Meredith turned red as she glared at the woman. "Meredith. The one and only. *Kam's* one and only too. Tell him I'll be back."

Meredith turned and pushed roughly out of the door making sure the door slammed behind her. The nerve of that woman, implying she was insane. Implying that Kam *wasn't* her boyfriend. Sure, they sort of took a break while she moved to California, but that was all in the past. None of the guys she'd met down in California could compare to Kam. All the men she'd dated had manicures, facials and had spent twice as much time in front of the mirror as she did. It was too daunting to date in L.A. Nah, she wanted a real man. A man who knew how to treat a woman. She wanted Kam, and no little ginger was going to get in her way either.

She drove over to Jane's bakery. Time to interrogate Jane and find out who that little pipsqueak was to Kam.

———

Wren watched as the door slammed shut and bit her lip. That woman was trouble with a capital T and Kam Matafeo was a dead man if Bailey found out there was a woman running around, calling herself his girlfriend. Bailey might be the calmest, most rational of the Downing siblings, *but she was still a Downing*, and she had a streak of passion in her that wouldn't mix well with a feisty blonde, who had just claimed her boyfriend. Wren winced at the picture in her mind of the cat fight, and turned to motion to Antonio.

"Gotta go talk to Rob for a minute. Scream for me if things get too crazy."

Antonio waved her off and she ran for Rob's office. She pushed through his door and of course, the man was on the phone. He was always on the phone. She crossed her arms and tapped her foot impatiently.

Rob raised an eyebrow at her foot and grinned before hanging up. "Sweetie, what is up? You look a little stressed," he said, getting up and walking around his desk so he could pull her into his arms.

Wren rolled her eyes and kissed him quickly, since there'd be not talking until he got one. "I just met Kam's girlfriend."

Rob laughed and shook his head. "Yeah, I've met her too. She's great. As a matter of fact, she's my sister. Wren, you're so weird."

Wren closed her eyes and prayed for patience. "Oh, you're paying for that. And no, not Bailey. Her name is Meredith, and she has a chip on her shoulder the size of Alaska and she announced to everyone that Kam was her man and blah *blah blah*. We've got a problem."

Rob's smile faded quickly and he stared at her with wide eyes. "*Meredith?* Oh, heavens no."

Wren nodded her head slowly. "Oh, yes, Rob. Bailey does not need this right now. She and Kam are just now beginning their relationship. Meredith is going to come in like a train wreck and do everything she can to get Kam back. This is so bad, Rob. Literally the worst timing ever."

Rob closed his eyes and covered his mouth with his hand. "I'll call Tate. He's good friends with Feke, and his wife Tawni is best friends with Meredith. Let me do a little digging. But you're right, Bailey does not need this right now. Yikes."

Wren hugged him quickly and kissed his cheek. "You're a good brother, but you can't fix everything. This is Kam's deal. He's the one who's going to have to figure out who he wants. Meredith or Bailey."

Rob frowned and shook his head. "He's the perfect man for Bailey. He better pick my sister."

Wren winced and patted his arm. "Sweetie, he might not."

Wren walked out of his office and hurried back to the kitchen. Why did disasters always come in threes. First one, Avery Brown's parole. Second one Meredith. What in the world was going to be the third? She frowned, not even wanting to think about it.

Chapter Seventeen

SUPPORT SYSTEM

Kam drove Bailey to her mom's house and turned off the Suburban. He turned and stared at Bailey and felt his heart twist. Her face said it all. Fear, dread and hope, all mixed together.

"Tell you what, let's get this over and then we can go back to your place and watch movies and eat popcorn. Whatever you want to do. We could go sit down by the beach too. You name it, we'll do it, but first things first."

Bailey nodded her head and reached over and grasped his hand. "Thanks, Kam. Please come with me."

Kam pursed his lips and glanced at the house. "Your mom might not want me there during this sensitive conversation."

Bailey stared at him, her blue eyes pleading with him. "But I do."

Kam sighed and got out of the car, walking around to open the door for her. She took his hand and jumped down, immediately melting into his side as they walked up the sidewalk to the front door. Bailey tried the door and found it unlocked, so she turned the knob and walked in, pulling him with her.

"*Mom?*" she called out, the house sounding hollow and empty.

Kam winced as he heard a door somewhere slam open and

running feet. Bailey stared up at him nervously, before Anne
Downing appeared, rushing toward them with her arms
outstretched.

"Baby!" Anne yelled, throwing her arms around her daughter's neck.

Kam closed his eyes as the pure emotion poured off of Anne,
surrounding Bailey and making her stagger under the weight of
her mother's arms and the weight of her pain on her behalf.

"Mom, I'm okay. *I'm okay*," she said, over and over and over,
as she patted Anne's back soothingly.

Anne shook her head, as new tears coursed down her face.
"Baby, how could you be? How could you be okay after that man
took advantage of you? You've been living with this weight on
your shoulders for six years. *How could you be okay?*"

Bailey closed her eyes and sighed, before pulling away from
her mom and stepping back. "Of course, there was damage, but
I'm living with it. I might have had problems trusting people,
and forming normal, healthy relationships, but I'm moving past
that. Kam knows a good therapist and I'm going to make an
appointment. I'm not perfect, but I'm okay. *Really*."

Anne wiped her eyes and stared at her daughter, as she shook
her head back and forth. "Why didn't you tell me?" she
whispered.

Kam winced and thought of all the times Bailey had already
heard those words today. The guilt must be crushing.

Bailey took in a deep breath and let it out slowly as she faced
her mom. "Because I was horribly ashamed, Mom. But at the
same time, I thought I was in love. I was pretty messed up and I
couldn't take that mess to you. I couldn't take it to anyone. It
was too heavy and gross and shameful and it was mine. But I'm
going to be free of it now. So, *please* . . . please stop hurting for
me, because I'm going to stop hurting now, too."

Kam stared at Bailey and wanted desperately to take her in
his arms but he settled for putting his hand on her waist, so she
could feel his support. Anne blinked and stared at Kam in

surprise. *"Kam?* What are you doing here with Bailey?" she asked, in confusion.

Bailey smiled faintly and looked up at him. "Mom, I'd like to introduce you to my *real* boyfriend. Kam Matafeo. Dean wasn't my boyfriend. Brogan wasn't my boyfriend. But I promise you, that this man is, and he's the best man I know."

Anne looked at him suspiciously and shook her head. "Bailey, you really do need therapy. This is crazy, all the men you've been dating lately."

Bailey grinned and then laughed a little, before turning and wrapping her arms around his waist. Kam grinned and held her securely in his arms. "Mrs. Downing, it's okay. I promise to take good care of your daughter. You have my word."

Anne sniffed and stared at him for a moment before nodding her head finally. "I should hope so. If Bailey comes home next week with someone else, I'm going to need a vacation."

Bailey snorted and let go of him to hug her mom one more time. "Mom, I'm going to take off, but I just wanted you to know that I was okay. I want you to relax and not worry about me anymore. This all happened six years ago, and it's over. Avery Brown is in jail and that's where he's staying."

Anne blinked, her eyes suddenly filled with pain. "I remember him," she whispered. "He would drop you off after softball practice, and I didn't think anything of it. I just thought he was such a nice man. I should have been suspicious of all the attention he paid you. I should have asked more questions. I should have known. And I didn't. Bailey, I'm so sorry, baby. I didn't protect you and I was your mom, and I didn't even think once that it was strange that this grown man was spending so much time with my daughter. I was a fool."

Kam's face hardened and his eyes turned cold, as he thought of the man who had taken advantage of not just Bailey's trust, but her whole family's trust. Bailey lowered her head and grasped her hands together.

"It's over, Mom. Let's put it in the past now."

Anne nodded her head and hugged Bailey one more time. "Okay, if that's what you want, Bailey. We'll try. I love you."

Bailey wiped her eyes and kissed her mom's cheek. "I love you too. I'll call you tomorrow, okay?"

Anne nodded and waved her hand, as Kam opened the door and they walked outside into the pale sunlight. Kam walked silently with her to the car, but paused before opening the door.

"You okay?"

Bailey looked up at him and threw her arms around his neck. Kam held her tightly, not letting go until she wanted him to. They stood there for almost five minutes, just holding each other. When Bailey finally lowered her arms, she looked up at him and smiled a little.

"You're official now. There's no going back. I've announced you to my mom. Doesn't that scare you a little?"

Kam smiled down at her and touched her cheek. "How could that scare me, when I'm right where I want to be?"

Bailey smiled bigger, her eyes warming as she looked at him. "I didn't know if I could ever really love a man again. I'm so relieved to find out, that not only can I love again, but I can love better and bigger and more, than I could have ever imagined."

Kam reached out and pulled her toward him. "No going back," he whispered, before leaning down and kissing her gently on the lips.

Bailey went up on her tiptoes and kissed him back, and Kam knew at that moment, that even though life could be hard and tragic and unfair, that sometimes there were moments that made up for all of it.

They drove back to her apartment and watched movies the rest of the day, and then had a pizza delivered. Kam ended up eating most of the pizza, and Bailey ended up falling asleep with her head resting on his chest.

Kam tucked her into bed and let himself out of her apartment late that night. And as he drove home, he smiled the entire way.

Chapter Eighteen

FIGHT CLUB

Bailey got up the next day, feeling better than she had in a long time. Better than she could ever remember. She threw her big dark glasses in the trash, and smiled as she walked out her door. No more hiding who she was. No more hiding behind walls. She was who she was, and people would just have to deal with her.

She was surrounded by co-workers and friends as soon as she walked in the building, and was touched by all the care and concern. When she got to her desk, she found cards and little vases of flowers. She put her hand over her heart at the outpouring of love and concern, and felt more touched than she'd ever been. She felt her cell phone vibrate and glanced down to see her boss's text.

In my office, please.

Bailey frowned slightly, but hurried to Jackson's office, knocking lightly before walking in and automatically shutting the door.

Jackson ran his hand over his balding head and frowned at her. "Are you ready to be back?"

Bailey nodded her head firmly, and clasped her hands behind her back to keep them from shaking. "I am."

He nodded his head thoughtfully and tapped the desk with

a pen. "We've had an overwhelming response to your article. Even more women have come forward, after reading what you wrote. And not just those accusing Avery Brown. Some women are accusing local ministers and other teachers and community leaders. You've created a groundswell. We had a meeting today and they want you to write a few more articles on your experience. Some possibilities would be, of course, how to prevent this from happening. And then the one *I* want you to write. Where do you go from here? How do you go on with life, after something like this happens. You could maybe talk about therapy and things that help you live with the memories and deal with the future. Something like that. And last but not least, how to prevent this from happening to innocent children."

Bailey frowned and stared at her feet. She thought that once she'd written her story, she was done. And now they wanted her to keep going. They wanted her turn over every last piece of her soul.

"And, if I say no?"

Jackson shrugged. "Then you say no, and I send you down to the school board to hammer them over more Common Core crap. It's up to you, Bailey. I know how hard this must be for you. I'm not going to push you. *Well*, I won't push you much. It's your decision. If you're done and you can't, then you can't. But if you can, then I think you should. I can pass this off to any of other writers, but with you personal experience and viewpoint, no one would be able to touch the level and depth you could, if you choose to."

Bailey sighed and rubbed her nose. "Can I think about it?"

Jackson smiled victoriously and gestured with his hand to the door. "Take the day. If it's a yes, I want an article tomorrow morning on my desk. Anything you want to write. It's your call."

Bailey smiled a little knowing how rare those words were. "Okay, then. I'll think about it and let you know. And thanks, Jackson."

Jackson nodded his head and sat back in his chair. "For what? Now get out of here and get to work."

Bailey smiled and left his office. Life really was okay. Life would be weird for a while, but it was going to go on. She went back to her desk and began going through her hundreds of emails. Two hours later, after getting through all of them, she leaned back in her chair and closed her eyes. *She had to write those articles.* Not for herself, but for all of the girls and boys who might benefit from her story. She really wanted to write the article that told the world that not only had she survived Avery Brown, she'd gone on to be happy and healthy. She had to write that article. And if she could save just one kid from going through what she had, then maybe it would all be worth it.

At one, she left the office and drove over to the restaurant. She couldn't wait to see Kam and tell him what she was going to do. She parked behind the restaurant and walked through the back door to the kitchen. It was so bright outside, it took her eyes a moment to adjust to the interior lights of the kitchen. She walked a few steps in and wondered why it was so quiet. She glanced around for Kam, and then stopped in her tracks. He was standing by the door, talking to a cute, little blond woman. Bailey frowned at how close they were standing, and wondered why the woman's hand was on Kam's bicep. It looked like an intimate conversation. *Very intimate.*

She walked closer, glaring now, as the woman now had her other hand on Kam's shoulder. *What the heck?* Kam began to shake his head and he reached up for the girl's hand, but before he could do anything, the woman snaked her arms around his neck and plastered her mouth to his.

Bailey gasped and stopped where she was. Kam pushed the woman away and glanced over in her direction, freezing when he saw her.

"*Bailey!*" he said, tearing the woman's arms away from him, and pushing her a few feet away. "Bailey, honey, this is *not* what it looks like."

Bailey felt an arm come around her and looked over to see Wren standing beside her, but she wasn't looking at her, she was glaring at the woman who was standing next to Kam with her chin in the air.

"*Kam?*" Bailey whispered, and shook her head as the image of the woman kissing him wouldn't leave her mind.

Pule walked up to her other side, and put his arm around her shoulders. "Bailey, when you dump my brother, I just want you to know that I'm available, and I would never cheat on you."

Kam's face turned hard and his eyes promised his little brother death, as he hurried to Bailey, grasping her arms and pulling her close to him. "She's an *ex*-girlfriend. Her name's Meredith and she just moved back from California. I guess she didn't realize that I have a new girlfriend now. I was just trying to explain that to her, when she started kissing me. I'm not cheating on you, Bailey. I would *never* do that to you," he said, sending a glare to Pule.

Bailey shuddered and Kam pulled her into his arms, ignoring the loud furious squawk, erupting behind him.

"Kam! We never really broke up. How can you say that to her?" the woman yelled, her voice turning loud and almost hysterical.

Bailey pulled back from Kam and looked around him at the furious woman. "You were together? *That* woman, is your ex-girl-friend?" she asked, wondering how Kam could date two people, so different from each other.

Kam glanced back over his shoulder at Meredith and winced. "She's really a great girl, and we had a lot of fun together, but we're better off being friends."

Meredith obviously heard what he said, and her eyes went wide and glazed. "Oh, is that right?" she whispered.

Kam frowned and turned around, staring cautiously at Meredith. "Meredith, I think you need to calm down. I think you should go home now. Please, do not make a scene. This is where I work, Meredith. Please consider that," Kam said soothingly, in a calm slow voice, as if he were talking to a rabid dog.

Meredith shook her head and reached for a large, metal bowl. She picked it up off the counter, and quicker than Bailey could have thought, she hurled it right at her. Kam reached out in front of her face, and blocked the bowl from crushing her nose, sending the bowl crashing to the floor.

Bailey gasped and then something lit inside of her. The fog and shock that had encased her, from seeing the man she loved, kissing another woman disappeared and she was suddenly filled with the desire to make Meredith cry.

With a roar of rage, Bailey grabbed a box of salt off the counter, and hurled it at Meredith. Meredith didn't have Kam standing there to block anything, and the box hit her squarely in the chest. Playing softball had given her a pretty good aim, if nothing else.

Meredith cried out in pain and looked at Kam for help. Kam held up his hands as Wren ran out the door.

"Bailey, Meredith, *please*. There is no need to resort to violence. Meredith, you shouldn't have thrown that bowl at Bailey. Now, Bailey, that was a good hit, but we're done now."

Pule crossed his arms over his chest and grinned between the two women. "Ladies, you do *not* need to be done. Just think Bailey, that woman just kissed your boyfriend. And Meredith? Are you going to let this little tramp, steal Kam away from you?"

Kam turned and stared at his little brother for a second, before he jumped on him, taking him down to the ground in a wrestling hold that had the eighteen year old squealing for mercy. Meredith took the opportunity to pick up an armful of potatoes, that Pule had been getting ready to peel, and she began systematically throwing them right at Bailey's head.

Bailey ducked two but got hit in the forehead with a large potato, that sent her spinning as she screamed in pain. She covered her head with her hand and then picked up one of the potatoes and threw it back, hitting Meredith in the stomach as hard as she could. Meredith yelled out a swear word, before bending over and groaning. Bailey saw her chance and ran forward, jumping on the woman, and taking her to the ground. She grabbed a hunk of Meredith's blond hair and yanked it, making the woman scream and grab at her wrist.

Meredith reached over and yanked a chunk of Bailey's hair in return, making Bailey screech in shock and pain. Kam threw Pule to the side and scrambled to reach Bailey. He attempted to pull Bailey away from Meredith, but she and Meredith were holding on with all of their strength. Meredith became even more enraged, as she realized Kam was trying to protect Bailey from her, and began calling Bailey horrible names, interspersed with swear words.

Bailey reached back and punched Meredith in the stomach, making her let go of her hair. Kam pulled her back to a safe distance, as Meredith started gagging.

"Come near Kam again and you'll regret it," Bailey said, glaring as Meredith slowly stood up and faced her again.

"Considering that he's mine, and he loves me, and not you, you can plan on it. Just face it, he was bored and you just happened to be convenient. He *doesn't* love you." Meredith said, flipping her tangled hair over her shoulder.

Bailey's eyes narrowed dangerously and she dove for Meredith again, but was lifted up and swung around, before she could reach her.

"Baby, *stop*. Please calm down," Kam said soothingly, as he held her tightly against his chest.

Meredith made a hissing sound, and dove for a stray potato, picking it up and aiming one last throw at the back of Bailey's head. Kam pulled her to the side just in time to avoid a concussion. Bailey growled and tore at Kam's hands as she fought to get to Meredith.

Just then, Taryn flew through the kitchen door and stopped as she saw Kam doing his best to restrain Bailey, and Meredith walking purposefully toward her with an evil look in her eyes.

Taryn narrowed her eyes and took in the situation quickly. She jumped in front of Meredith and looked her up and down. "Kam, please tell me this isn't your ex-girlfriend. I thought you said she was pretty?" she said, with a sneer.

Meredith's rage switched to Taryn, and she yelled as she launched herself at her. Taryn ducked Meredith's claws and gave her a quick jab in the side, making her stumble and gasp in pain.

"Stay out if this. This is between me and your trashy, little sister. If you don't back off, I promise you'll get hurt too," Meredith said, in a hoarse voice.

Taryn's lips peeled back in a snarl. "*You hurt my sister?*" she hissed, and moved toward Meredith menacingly. "Do you want to know what happened to the last girl, who thought she could mess with Bailey?"

Meredith massaged her side as she stared at Taryn with a wary look in her eyes. "*What?* Some girl pushed her down and scraped her knee? When was it? Kindergarten? Did you run and tell your mommy? Really impressive, psycho. Now get out of my way, so I can finish teaching your sister a lesson."

Taryn blinked her eyes slowly, as she removed her earrings and slipped them in her pocket.

"*Taryn*," Kam said warningly, but Taryn ignored him.

Taryn slipped off her high heels and cracked her knuckles. "It wasn't kindergarten and I was a senior in high school. Lucky for me, they didn't charge me as an adult," she said, in a cold voice, that had Bailey grinning proudly.

Meredith put her chin in the air and shook her head. "All talk. Look at you. What were you two? Pageant queens?"

Taryn laughed evilly. "As a matter of fact," she said.

Meredith rolled her eyes and walked forward, pushing Taryn hard in the chest with her finger. "Mind your own business. This is between me and her," she said, poking her again.

Taryn didn't even hesitate, she knocked Meredith's hands off and pushed her so hard, the woman went flying backwards, landing on the floor.

Brogan rushed forward to help Meredith stand, but she shook him off. Taryn laughed at Meredith's shocked expression, and turned around to check on Bailey, walking towards her with a worried frown on her face.

Bailey gasped out a warning, as Meredith leaped forward and grabbed the back of Taryn's hair, pulling her backwards so hard, that Taryn lost her balance and landed on her back. Quicker than Bailey could have imagined, Taryn was on her feet again, snarling something that had Bailey's eyes widening. Meredith began to look worried, her eyes darting for the door. She backed up a few feet, but Taryn was too furious now. She pulled back her right arm and sent it flying into Meredith's face, making Bailey wince, Kam groan and Brogan grin proudly.

Pule, Ramon and Cynthia gasped and started talking loudly over each other. "*Holy crap,* Taryn," Brogan muttered, as he rushed to help Meredith stand up. Cynthia grabbed a paper towel and handed it to Meredith, as Pule and Ramon and Antonio circled around, waiting for someone to re-start the fight.

Taryn massaged her hand as Brogan left Meredith to walk toward her slowly. He watched her with a slight grin around his mouth, as she slipped her high heels back on. "What is it about the Downings, that if there's a fight somewhere, one of you is in the middle of it?"

Taryn smiled and shrugged. "You know I don't let anyone mess with my family. She thought she could hurt Bailey. *Idiot.* Call 911, Brogan. I want this woman arrested for assault."

Kam let go of Bailey and rushed forward, grabbing Taryn's arms. "Taryn, I know it looks bad, and I know this woman is slightly crazy, but she's my ex-girlfriend, and as a favor, I'd like to talk to her outside for a moment instead of calling the police. She was shocked to find out that I have a new girlfriend, and didn't take it well. Bailey didn't like the way Meredith was handling the situation and things got violent. Please, Taryn?"

Bailey stared at her big sister and watched her eyes go from hot rage to exasperated amusement. *Phew*. She did not want to talk to the police about her part in this mess. Talk about embarrassing.

"Fine, Kam, but anymore of your ex-girlfriends attack my sister, and I'm getting my taser out."

Bailey glanced over at Meredith warily, and saw that she was holding the paper towels to her mouth, as she began to cry. Bailey winced and looked away from the woman's humiliation. Her dignity was a little tattered, she didn't need anyone gloating.

Kam grimaced and looked back at her with dark serious eyes, before taking Meredith by the arm and walking her quickly outside. Taryn walked over and pulled Bailey into her arms for a quick hug, before letting her go.

"You okay?" she asked worriedly.

Bailey nodded quickly, before Taryn could get mad again. Pule walked over and slung his arm around her shoulders, smiling at her with respect in his eyes.

"Taryn, you missed it. Bailey went crazy and attacked Meredith. Best thing I've seen in years," he said, with a proud grin.

Taryn laughed and looked Bailey up and down. Bailey glanced at herself and groaned. She looked like a mess. She looked exactly the way you'd expect someone to look, after brawling on the floor.

"I knew she had it in her. People have wondered if she was adopted, but right here, today, she just proved beyond any doubt, she's a Downing."

Brogan grinned and walked over to Bailey, and touched the large, red mark on her forehead. "Looks like you're going to have a bad bruise. Why don't I get you an ice pack?"

Pule still wanted to relive every moment of the fight and sighed happily. "Dang, Bailey, I had a feeling you had a violent streak, but the way you yanked on that woman's hair should be an Olympic sport. I bet you a million dollars, she has a bald patch," he said, with a grin.

Bailey pushed her hair out of her face and laughed a little.

"And this, coming from the man who told Meredith, I was a little tramp?"

Taryn turned slowly around and pinned Pule with a cold glare. "What did you call my sister?"

Pule's eyes went wide with fear and he held up his hands. "I was caught up in the moment. I had no idea what I was saying. Of course, Bailey isn't a tramp. She's the woman my brother loves, and as Kam's brother, I would die to protect her honor," he said quickly, as Brogan moved to stand between him and Taryn.

Bailey sighed and touched her forehead gingerly. "It's okay, Taryn, Kam pounded him for it, which gave me the opportunity to jump Meredith, so it's all good."

Taryn laughed and stared at Bailey with surprised respect in her eyes. "Well, it's good to know you can handle yourself. I'd still rather you didn't have to though. Next time she shows her face at The Iron Skillet, she's all mine."

Wren rushed into the kitchen, pulling Rob with her and paused as she looked around for Meredith. "*Wait.* I thought there was a fight going on?" she said, as Rob raised an eyebrow and laughed.

"Yeah right. When you said Bailey was going to fight some-one, I knew you had to be kidding. Taryn? Sure, why not. But Bailey would never hurt anyone on purpose."

Bailey grinned as Taryn and Pule competed with each other to tell Rob all the gory details. Rob frowned darkly, as he pulled her over and checked her forehead and ran his hands down her arms.

"*Seriously?* You did all that?" he asked, still sounding doubtful.

Bailey shrugged. "I *am* your sister, Rob. Jeez, you act like I'm a wimp. I see a woman kissing my boyfriend, there's going to be consequences."

Rob's eyes lit up and he laughed, kissing her on the head gently. "And where is Kam now? Shouldn't he be here with you, kissing your bruises and begging for your forgiveness?

Brogan brought over an ice pack and held it gently to Bailey's head. "I believe he's in the parking lot, trying to explain to his ex that she shouldn't mess with his girlfriend."

Bailey winced as she put her hand over the ice pack. "Well, even if I'm not tough enough to scare her off, my sister will."

Taryn kissed her gently on the cheek and touched her hair. "Love you, Bailey. Stay for lunch if you can."

Bailey smiled, agreeing readily and talked to her family and Brogan for a few more minutes, as she waited for Kam to come back in the kitchen. When he didn't, she set her ice pack down and walked to the back door.

"*Bailey* . . ." Rob said warningly.

Bailey flipped her hair over her shoulder and ignored him. She opened the door a crack and looked out into the parking lot. She saw Kam standing with Meredith, by his old white Suburban. Bailey felt her heart squeeze as she saw Kam run his hand down Meredith's hair. Meredith was crying hard, and her shoulders were shaking, as she shook her head back and forth and said the word *no,* over and over.

Bailey shut the door and felt horrible all of a sudden. She turned around and saw that Rob, Wren, Taryn and Brogan were all standing silently, watching her worriedly. She frowned and looked at her feet. "It looks like her heart's breaking, and Kam is being very gentle with her. I feel like crap now," she muttered, lifting the ice pack back to her forehead.

Rob walked forward and pulled her into his arms. "Sweetie, Kam loves *you* now. Meredith chose to leave him. Don't feel bad. Now, let's go into the dining room and we'll all have lunch together."

Bailey smiled faintly and nodded, following Rob and Taryn to an intimate table for four. Bailey didn't even glance at the menu and just told Brogan to bring her anything Wren felt like making her. Rob and Taryn tried to get her to smile again, but the memory of the gentle way Kam had touched Meredith's hair, wouldn't stop playing and replaying through her mind. What if

Kam and Meredith were meant to be together, and she'd just messed everything up?

Bailey groaned lightly and rested her head in her hands, as she put herself in Meredith's shoes. She knew how she felt about Kam, and knew how she'd feel if Kam moved onto someone else. *She'd be dying.*

She felt a hand on her shoulder and looked up to see Kam, standing beside her with a concerned frown on his face. "Ah, *wow*. She got you good," he muttered, his mouth tightening, as he gently touched the raised red skin on her forehead.

Bailey stared at him solemnly as he sat down next to her. Rob cleared his throat and grabbed Taryn's hand, helping her up. "I just remembered Taryn and I have a meeting with one of our suppliers. Gotta run," he said, and pulled Taryn away from the table.

Kam sighed and stared at her with a worried frown. "Did she just mess up everything between us?" he asked softly.

Bailey looked away from him and crossed her legs, leaning back in her chair, further away from him. "What do you mean?" she asked, not answering the question.

Kam moved closer to her and put his hands on her knees as he leaned toward her. "I can see your eyes, Bailey. You're closing yourself off from me. You're putting up your barriers again. Don't do that. Don't push me away."

Bailey licked her lips and looked up at the ceiling, so she didn't have to look at Kam's sad and thoughtful eyes. "Kam, I'm not blind. I saw her. She loves you. You two have a history and I got the distinct impression, it's not over between you two."

Kam sat up, his jaw turning hard and his eyes narrowing. "And now, you want to throw away what we have together? Is that it, Bailey? You're going to step back from me?"

Bailey let out a shaky breath and let herself look at Kam. He looked furious. He looked upset. "I don't want to, Kam," she said quietly.

Kam reached over and pulled her chair closer to his, before

leaning over so they were nose to nose. "Don't back away from me, Bailey. I told you I loved you and I meant it. You told me you loved me, and I believe you. Don't let what just happened, mess that up."

Bailey swallowed and slowly reached up with both of her hands to touch Kam's jaw, before moving to run her hands down his hair, pulling his ponytail over his shoulder. "Did you not notice me fighting for you?" she asked, with a small smile.

Kam closed his eyes as if in relief, and put his hand behind her neck pulling her in as he lowered his mouth to hers, sealing her lips with his, as she wrapped her arms around his neck. Kam took his time kissing her, until the clearing of throats brought her back to reality. Reality was, Kam was kissing her breathless in the middle of her brother's restaurant, and this probably wasn't the place for such a public display of affection.

She pulled back and kissed Kam's cheek before whispering in his ear. "We're causing a scene."

Kam lifted his head and glared at all of the people surrounding him and then sighed. "Fine, I can wait. Bailey, are you and me good?"

Bailey couldn't resist kissing Kam along his jaw before answering. "I think so, but this should really be a warning to you, Kam. Me and your ex-girlfriends are not a good combination."

Kam grinned down at her, before kissing her red bruised forehead softly. "Who knew Bailey Downing, was the type of woman to get in a catfight, over the man she loves?"

Bailey grinned and yanked on Kam's hair. "*You*, now. Any other women I should know about?" she asked lightly.

Kam shook his head before picking up her hand and kissing the back. "None. You're the only woman for me. You're the only woman I love."

Bailey stared into Kam's serious brown eyes and nodded her head. She believed him. "Okay, then. Will Meredith be back? Does she understand that you and I are together now?"

Kam looked away, his eyebrows knit together in a dark

frown, and she knew the answer, but she waited for him to say it. "Meredith is an awesome girl, but she has a stubborn streak. She um, has decided that she's going to win me back. It's possible that she might show up here again."

Bailey's eyebrows shot up and she sat back from Kam, her blue eyes shining with anger. "Oh, really," she breathed out, feeling adrenaline spike through her blood again.

Kam sat back and grinned at her. "You are so gorgeous when you're mad, you know that? You should see yourself right now. Your hair's all wild and your eyes are this dangerous, electric blue. This might be incredibly shallow of me, but seeing you jealous and violent is . . ." he paused, and looked away.

Bailey frowned and nudged his foot with hers. "What? Is what?" she prodded.

Kam cleared his throat and shook his head, his eyes dark and soft. "It's incredibly . . . um, *cute*. Listen, I gotta get back to the kitchen, but finish your lunch and come say goodbye before you leave."

Bailey nodded and kissed him lightly on the lips before he stood up. "And Kam? Please don't kill Pule."

Kam's eyes turned bright and hard and his hands clenched into fists. "That kid is getting what he deserves," he said.

Bailey swallowed and stood up quickly to throw her arms around Kam's neck. "I'll try and forget the fact that I came to see you this afternoon, and found another woman kissing you, if you promise not to kill your brother."

Kam groaned and wrapped his arms around her waist, holding her close as he stared down into her eyes. "But, I really need to," he said plaintively.

Bailey grinned and kissed him again. "For me?"

Kam grinned and kissed her back. "Only for you then," he said, letting her go and walking away.

Bailey watched him go and smiled softly. Meredith might want him, but he was hers. Completely.

Chapter Nineteen

PURGING

The next day, Bailey took her laptop and went down to the beach. She couldn't be at the office with so many people surrounding her, and she didn't want to be home with what she was going to write. She didn't want to pollute her apartment with old memories. She needed to be somewhere cleansing and pure. She needed to feel the energy of the water surround her as she purged the final bits of damage from her soul, for the good of some nameless person, who might read her thoughts and find a little strength in them. If she could, then others could too and that was why she was doing what she was doing.

She started by writing about how she felt leaving high school behind, and how she had assumed as soon as she graduated, and left the place that held all the bad memories, that she'd be free from Avery, *but that hadn't happened.* His memory had followed her to college and he'd followed her on every date she went on. Six years of trying to be free and having his memory hang on to her like a leech, sucking any possibility of having a normal and healthy relationship away. She then wrote about how dumb she felt for not getting counselling sooner. How dumb she felt for waiting six years, to open the bandage over her heart, just to realize that she still hadn't healed the way she'd hoped to.

Abuse doesn't just disappear. It lingers like a bad taste in your mouth, and it sucked the light out of your life. It was almost as if, every memory that stayed with her, was Avery continuing to abuse her. *And she'd allowed it.*

She then wrote about her decision to fully commit to purging her life of Avery Brown. Purging her life of the shame she'd been carrying around with her, like a bright red scarlet A on her chest. Purging her life of the man who should have never been in her life. She wrote about taking the necessary steps to making sure he was gone for good.

Number one, talking about it. Talking about it and writing about it, until her soul was free. Second, choosing to love again. Being brave and refusing to allow Avery to tarnish good and pure love, that everyone should have the right to. Third, getting professional help to make sure she was on the right path. And four, talking to other survivors and helping others break free from their scarlet letters.

She sat on the weathered gray, wooden bench, as the water crashed on the rocks and read over what she'd written. She wiped a few tears away and smiled. They were good tears. They meant she was feeling again. She stood up and reached her hands to the sky and smiled, before hiking back to her car and driving home. She emailed Jackson the article and then went for a run. She ran by a gym and wondered if she should start working out. If she had to deal with Meredith again, she needed to be in top shape. Who knew that taking on a beautiful Samoan boyfriend, could be so dangerous?

She grinned and kept running. With Taryn as her sister, she probably wouldn't get the chance to face Meredith again. It was nice having so many people ready to jump in to defend you. Nice, but annoying sometimes. She kind of liked standing on her own two feet. She reached up and touched her bruised forehead and winced. Meredith packed some heat though. Maybe having Taryn backing her up, wasn't such a bad idea.

She ran down the road Belinda's Bakery was on and grinned.

She'd stop and beg for a cup of water, and see if Jane was around. She needed to get some background on Kam's ex and Jane was the perfect woman for the job. She ran up the stairs and pushed through the door, smiling at the sound of the bell and the instant smell of heavenly chocolate.

Jane and Kit were behind the counter, helping a man pick out what he wanted. She waved at Jane and Jane's eyes went big, as she ran around the counter.

"I've been calling you and texting you for two days! Why haven't you called me back?" she demanded, her hands on her hips.

Bailey winced and held up her hands. "I've been getting so many calls lately, I decided to turn my phone off. *Sorry.* What's up?"

Jane stared at her with her mouth open. "*What's up?* Are you crazy? What's up is Meredith. What's up is the article I read Tuesday. What's up is that we're friends, and you haven't returned my calls."

Bailey bit her lip as Jane went on for a few more minutes. Kit waved off the elderly man and then joined them, steering them both to a table by the window and pointing to the two chairs.

"Sit, you two. Now work this out. Thirsty, Bailey?"

Bailey nodded gratefully and listened to Jane lambast her for a few more minutes before Jane stood up and walked around the table, throwing her arms around her shoulders and hugging her tightly.

"I'm so sorry you had to go through what you did. If you ever need someone to talk to, Layla was a social worker and she's seen it all. She volunteers down at the battered women's shelter, and she sees a lot of women who have been abused. Do you mind if I give her your phone number?"

Bailey bit her lip and nodded. "That would be great. Kam made an appointment for me with a therapist he knows, who helped Tate when he was a teenager, but that's not until next week. I'd really like to talk to someone sooner than that."

Jane sat back down and smiled, happy now that she'd said what she had to. "Now, what are you going to do about Meredith?"

Bailey shrugged and smiled as Kit brought her a cup of water. "Well, I ripped out most of her hair and threw a potato at her. So, I think I've already done what I wanted to. Why?"

Jane and Kit stared at her silently for a moment before Kit grabbed a chair and pulled it over to the table. Jane ran over to the door and changed the sign to CLOSED, and then hurried back.

Kit pointed at her. "Talk."

Bailey grinned and went over everything. She started with her relationship with Kam and the family dinner on Sunday, and ended with seeing Kam talking so gently with Meredith in the parking lot.

Kit shook her head and sighed before glancing at Jane. Jane ran her hands through her hair and looked worried. "That's one of the reasons I've been trying to call you, you brat. Meredith came by yesterday and wanted to know everything about you. Tate had already given me a head's up that Kam liked you, but I wasn't sure how serious you were, so I just told her that things were casual. Sorry."

Kit pushed Jane in the shoulder and Jane looked at her reproachfully. Bailey held up her hand. "It's not your fault, Jane. You didn't know. But now that Meredith knows, now that Kam has laid it out for her, and now that she and I had a knock down fight on the kitchen floor at The Iron Skillet, will she back off?"

Kit shook her head. "Jane's friends with Meredith, but personally, I think the woman is a brat. I bet you a million dollars, she makes it her life's quest to get Kam back."

Jane grimaced and nodded her head. "Kit's right. I love Meredith and she's my friend, but I love you too and you're my friend, so I'm going to be honest with you. Buy some mace."

Bailey took a sip of water and stared up at the ceiling. "Why is life never easy?"

Kit grinned and ran her hands over her still small stomach. "If it was easy, it wouldn't be so fun. Now, tell us about Kam. What made you fall for him instead of pursuing Dean?"

Bailey blinked in surprise at hearing Dean's name. She'd almost forgotten about the man. "I'll be honest, Kam kind of scared me at first. The way he looked at me, you know? He was never rude or anything, but sometimes he would look at me with those dark, intense eyes of his, and it was like he could reach out and touch me with just a look."

Kit sighed and smiled, while Jane grinned and leaned her chin on her hands. "Go on," she urged.

Bailey took another sip of water and looked out the window. "I could always tell when he came into the room without looking. There's this electric current between us that connects us, somehow. And last Saturday when he kissed me again . . ."

"Wait," Jane said, holding up her hands. "Uh, uh. *Again?*"

Bailey laughed and crossed her legs, getting comfortable. "Well, at Taryn's birthday party, I sort of went out of my way to distract him from Wren, so Rob could get her back. Well, he realized what was going on, and kissed the stuffing out of me. He was kind of mad at the time, but *holy cow*, that man can kiss," she said, laughing softly at the memory.

Kit sat up and motioned with her hands. "You're killing me! Then what?"

Bailey sat forward and smiled. "Well, Saturday when he came into the restaurant and I was trying to persuade Brogan to be my fake boyfriend, to get my mom off my back because of Dean, he dragged me back to Rob's office and kissed me until my knees melted. *Best. Kiss. Of. My. Life.*"

Jane grinned and shook her head. "It must run in the family. So, that was that. You and Kam. Chemistry, heat and now you two are together, and you have a crazy ex-girlfriend after you. Your life isn't boring, have you noticed that?"

Bailey laughed and put her cup on the table. "I'm beginning too."

Kit tilted her head and stared at Bailey. "So, I hope you don't mind me making an observation, but all of the guys you've dated, have been like Dean. Successful, white collar, suit-wearing, MBA toting, upwardly mobile guys. They've all been cookie cutter guys, that could be on the cover of GQ magazine. Kam doesn't fit any mold. He doesn't wear suits, he has long hair and a pretty impressive tattoo on his arm, for the world to see. He's not your type at all, Bailey. You're not going to get tired of him after the newness wears off, and set him free in exchange for a suit and tie are you?"

Bailey glared at Kit and uncrossed her legs, so she could sit up. "I'll admit, I had some hang ups when it came to Kam. We come from different cultures. He has long hair and has the build of an MMA fighter. He's not a college graduate and he works for my brother. We are different and I thought that that would be a problem for me, and that's one of the reasons I was so hesitant to go for him, but after being with Kam, I've realized that none of that matters. I love his long hair. I'd be devastated if he cut it. I love his beautiful, brown skin and I even like his tattoo. I love him. All of him," she said simply.

Jane smiled dreamily and Kit grinned and patted her hand. "It's settled then. Meredith's out. You're in. I can tell the real deal, when I see it, and girl, you have it bad."

Jane nodded her head and crossed her arms over her chest. "You're in love with Kam Matafeo. I'm going to design a new cupcake for the occasion in honor of a beautiful love story."

Bailey laughed and stood up. "Jane, you are the best friend a girl could have."

"*And the best wife.*"

Bailey, Kit and Jane turned around to see Tate Matafeo leaning against the counter, with a big smile on his face. Bailey blushed, wondering how much he'd heard of their conversation. Jane jumped up and walked over to her husband, wrapping her arms around his waist as he leaned down and kissed her lightly.

"So, you love my brother?"

Bailey turned an even brighter red, as Kit stood up next to her, and put her arm through hers. She nodded her head quickly. "Yes, yes I do," she said softly.

Tate let go of his wife and walked over to stand in front of her, and then surprised her by hugging her warmly, patting her on the back before stepping back.

"Then, that's good enough for me. Welcome to the family," he said, with a happy grin on his face.

Bailey relaxed and laughed a little. "Wait, I thought you were cousins?"

Tate shrugged and grabbed Jane's hand in his. "We're more brothers than cousins. Does he know you love him?"

Bailey bit her lip and looked away feeling embarrassed. "Well, I've never told any man that I loved him before, but I can't seem to stop telling Kam."

Tate grinned and nodded his head. "That answers my question."

Jane beamed at her and looked up at Tate, before whispering in his ear. Whatever she said, made Tate grin and he nodded his head. "Well, ladies, I just stopped by for a cupcake break, but I've gotta head out. Jane, walk me to my car?"

Jane grabbed his hand, and they headed back towards the kitchen. Kit grinned at them before turning back to her. "I do believe ,my little sister is now dreaming of having you as a cousin in law."

Bailey laughed and pushed her chair into the table, before walking toward the front door. "Let's not get ahead of ourselves, Kit. We just started dating."

Kit followed her to the door and opened it for her, switching the sign to OPEN. "Well, just in case you're wondering, Jane and I are experts at picking out wedding dresses and planning receptions."

Bailey felt her heart rate speed up and she smiled and escaped as fast as she could, jumping into a run as soon as she hit the sidewalk. *Weddings? Dresses? Receptions?* Holy cow. She ran as fast as she could, all the way home and leaned up against her door, panting as sweat poured down her forehead. She might be ready to love Kam, but *marrying* Kam, was a little overwhelming.

She found the energy to open her door, and made it to the bathroom where she turned on the shower and stayed there for twenty minutes. Hydrotherapy. The best therapy.

When she got out, she cleared the mirror with a towel and stared at the now faintly purplish bruise, forming on her forehead. If Meredith's aim had been better she could have a broken nose or a black eye. Bailey glared at the bruise and almost hoped Meredith did come back by the restaurant.

"Bailey," she said, talking to herself in the mirror, "You are not a barbarian. You are a logical and mature adult, who solves problems through discussion and compassion. You will not beat up Meredith, no matter how many potatoes she throws at you," she said sternly.

Then she grinned. If Meredith threw even one little green onion at her, she was toast. She blow dried her hair and then went over all of her voicemails she'd missed over the last couple days. There were forty-seven. Twenty of them from her brother, sister and mother and ten from Kam, and the rest from Jane and co-workers.

And one from Dean Hogan.

She listened to the message from Dean and frowned before replaying it.

"Hey, Bailey, this is Dean. I read the article you wrote for the paper and I want to get together for lunch soon. As you know, I'm a psychologist and I have a group of women I work with, who are survivors of sexual abuse. I was wondering if you would be interested in talking to them? Sometimes we have guest speakers and I find that it helps. I'd also like to take you to dinner soon. For personal reasons though. Call me."

Bailey stared at her phone with a frown. After telling her he wanted to date as many women as possible, he wanted to take her out again? She shook her head and decided to think about calling him back. The thought of getting up in front of women and talking about her experiences sent chills down her spine. Writing, she could do. *Speaking in front of people?* Not so much.

She cleaned up her apartment and then wandered into the kitchen to see what she could make for dinner, when she heard a light knock on her door. She looked through the peephole and grinned, before pulling the door open and jumping into Kam's open arms.

"*Kam!* What are you doing here? You're working tonight."

Kam grinned and kissed her before carrying her into the apartment and kicking the door shut with his foot. "I have an hour break, and wanted to spend it with you, of course."

Bailey dropped down to the floor and then remembered she had absolutely no makeup on, and she was wearing her most comfortable yoga pants and her favorite faded and stained t-shirt. She turned to run to the bathroom, when Kam grabbed her hand and stopped her.

"Hey, I just got here. Where are you going?"

Bailey blushed and tried to pull her hand free. "I just need to put on a little cover up and a few other things," she said, twisting her head away.

Kam picked her up again and carried her to the couch, where he sat down with her in his lap. "I've never seen you without makeup before. You're gorgeous."

Bailey looked at him doubtfully and tried one more time to twist away. "Just give me five minutes," she began, before Kam was kissing her and she forgot all about makeup and how she looked.

Kam lifted his head and smoothed her hair back with his hand as he stared down at her. "I love this face. Now, tell me about your day."

Bailey relaxed and told him about the article she wrote, and how it had made her feel and then she mentioned running past the bakery and stopping in. Kam's eyes brightened and his smile grew wider, as he played with her hair, twisting it around his finger.

"Tate came by the restaurant today, and wanted to know all about the fight between you and Meredith. He mentioned seeing you at the bakery, and he asked me how serious we were."

Bailey blushed, remembering her very frank conversation with Tate and grabbed a throw pillow to hide her face behind. Kam slowly pulled the cushion away and grinned at her. "Any reason, he'd be asking me something like that?"

Bailey shook her head and bit her lip. "He kind of asked me the same question in a roundabout way."

Kam nodded, his eyes bright and warm. "And what did you say?"

Bailey twisted off Kam's lap and landed on the floor where she attempted to crawl away, but he was next to her in a second, his large leg, capturing her hips so she couldn't move. "What was that? I couldn't hear you."

Bailey giggled and gave up, hiding her face in her arms. "He asked me if you knew I loved you, and I told him something like, I thought you did."

Kam shook his head. "No, I want to hear your exact words. Tate said it was sweet."

Bailey groaned but turned her head to look at him. She sighed and reached over to pull Kam's long dark hair through her hand. "I said, I'd never told another man I loved him before, but that I couldn't seem to stop telling you that I did. Tate seemed to accept my answer. He's kind of protective of you, you know. I think he wanted to make sure I really loved you, and that I wasn't using you as arm candy."

Kam laughed and grabbed her, twisting her over his body, so she was on her back and he could look down at her face. "No one's ever called me arm candy before."

Bailey grinned and followed the line of his tattoo with her finger. "Anyone who has seen you do the Haka, would agree with me, I'm afraid. You're beautiful," she said softly.

Kam leaned his head on his hand, as he traced her face with

his finger. "I don't know if I agree with you, but I like that you think so."

Bailey and Kam talked for forty-five minutes, before he had to head back to the restaurant. No mention of Meredith was made. And as she shut the door on Kam, she realized she hadn't told him about Dean's request to take her to dinner. She frowned as she locked the door, and told herself she'd tell him tomorrow. They'd both been in such a good mood, that she hadn't wanted to change that. There'd been too much drama and sadness lately. She just wanted to enjoy time with Kam, without anyone ruining it.

She went to bed that night with a smile on her face. Falling in love with Kam had been the best thing that had ever happened to her, and she didn't want anything or anyone ruining that.

Chapter Twenty

FRIENDS AND FOES

Meredith stared at Jane across the table, as they shared a plate of nachos. "So, what you're saying is, that Kam and this girl, *Bailey,* are good together, and that I should back off, because you think Kam is genuinely happy with her."

Jane nodded her head cautiously, as she smiled gently at Meredith. "I know this is painful and it hurts, but *yes,* Kam is happy now. After you left Meredith, he was really down and sad. And Meredith, you *did* break up with him. You can't change history to suit yourself."

Meredith glared at Jane and crossed her arms over her chest. "Whose friend are you, Jane? It's almost like you *want* Bailey to be with Kam. You're *my* friend, and you're supposed to be on *my* side."

Jane held up her hands and shook her head. "Meredith, listen, I am your friend, but I'm Bailey's friend too."

Meredith's mouth fell open in shock. "Do you know what she did to me? She threw a potato at my stomach, and tried to rip my hair out. She tackled me like she was a linebacker. That woman is evil and insanely possessive!"

Jane lifted her eyebrow doubtfully at her. "That's not exactly how I heard it happened. I heard that you were the one who started it, and I saw Bailey, Meredith. The potato you threw at her forehead, left a huge bruise. And I'd be possessive and mad too, if I walked in and found some strange woman kissing Tate. I think she had a very normal reaction."

Meredith turned red in the face, and looked away from Jane. "What did you expect me to do, Jane? I come back home, and find that not only has Kam moved on, but now he's dating some pretty, little Barbie doll and he's forgotten all about me. I figured he needed a little reminder."

Jane winced and took a sip of her virgin margarita. "Meredith, let's do this. Let's put this relationship with Kam to rest, and focus on getting you settled and dating and socializing again. You've only been home for a few days now."

Meredith shook her head and stood up. "I can't believe this. You're *my* friend, and you're turning your back on me. Jane, if it was you, and you wanted to get Tate back from some little, witch, I'd do everything I could to help you, and here you are telling me to forget about Kam. Maybe I shouldn't have even come back home. I've not only lost Kam, but I've lost you too. Well, too bad Jane, because I'm not the kind of woman who gives up so easy."

Jane turned and watched Meredith stomp out of the restaurant, and frowned sadly, her heart breaking for her friend. Meredith was pretty good at guilt trips too, and she felt bad knowing that Meredith thought she was a crummy friend. But when she thought about Bailey and the large bruise on her forehead, and the bravery she had shown in admitting that she loved Kam, she had to admit that her loyalties were firmly with Kam and Bailey on this one. She picked up a smothered nacho and sighed, because Meredith was not going to make it easy on them.

She motioned for the waiter and handed him her credit card, before taking out her phone and texting Tate.

Meredith won't stop. Kam's in trouble.

A few minutes later her phone vibrated. *Meredith will stop. She can't break up true love.*

Jane smiled and sighed as she stood up and grabbed her jacke off the back of her chair. Tate was right. Things would be fine.

Maybe.

Chapter Twenty-One

BREAKING UP

Bailey spent the next few days writing more articles, being interviewed by the local TV news channels, and running back and forth between her apartment and the restaurant. She used to drop by Rob's restaurant two or three times a week. Now she was there two or three times a day. Even seeing Kam for a few minutes or grabbing lunch with him would turn a hard grim day, into a good day. That and she was getting addicted to the feel of his arms around her. With Kam's arms around her, she'd never felt so safe or strong. With Kam's support and love, she could do anything. She could write her truth and know that he'd never turn away from her. She could speak in front of cameras, knowing that thousands of people would see her and know what had happened to her, and she could do it, because she knew that the people who truly knew her and loved her, were standing right there with her.

She was becoming a new person, now that she had opened herself to love. She was stronger, happier and more open than she'd ever been before. She opened the door to the restaurant and glanced at her watch. Saturdays were their busiest days, but she hadn't seen Kam all day, and she was dying for even a glance at him.

Brittany looked a little stressed as the line of people filled the foyer. She waved and gave her a commiserating look, before bypassing the line and walking back to the kitchen. She pushed through the door and frowned as she saw how quickly everyone was moving. Not the best time for a girlfriend to stop by. She waved at Kam and he grinned at her, before wiping his forehead with his arm.

"Hey, Gorgeous. I won't bug you, but I just had to stop by and get a kiss and tell you I love you. I was going through withdrawals," she said, kissing him quickly as his arm wrapped around her waist automatically.

He grinned and pulled her back, kissing her again, much more slowly. "You could never bug me. And kissing you is the best break I could have. I'm glad you stopped by. Mom wants you to come over for dinner tomorrow. That okay?"

Bailey nodded and waved at Wren as she zoomed past. "Of course, it's okay. Let me know what I can bring."

Kam nodded and kissed her again, before letting her go with a grin. "Stay for dinner and I'll come out later, and take a break with you."

Bailey nodded and blew him a kiss, before walking out of the kitchen. She headed down the hallway to her brother's office and poked her head inside. He was on the phone, but as soon as he saw her, he waved her inside. She sat down and crossed her legs, checking her messages as she waited for him to finish up. Five minutes later, he put his cell phone down and smiled happily at her.

"Just the person I wanted to see. Wren refuses to go see this new venue for the reception. She says it's too big, but I think it's perfect. We're running out of time, and it's one of the only places that can fit all the people, I want to come. Come see it with me. It'll only take an hour."

Bailey winced and looked away from her brother's hopeful face, remembering her vow to Wren. "Rob, buddy, *listen*. Wren has a touch of social anxiety disorder. She *hates* crowds. She especially hates *big* crowds. She just wants a little intimate wedding, without all of your baseball buddies getting drunk and ruining everything. She wants it here at the restaurant. You gotta let this go, Rob."

Rob frowned at her and crossed his arms over his chest. "Wren won't even notice all the people, because she's going to be so happy. Besides, I'll be right by her side the entire night. This is my reception too, Bailey. I want this to be the party of a lifetime. She'll love it once I get her there. You'll see."

Bailey frowned and shook her head. "It's not about you, Rob. It's about you *and* Wren and Wren will hate that. Let it go. Invite all of our family and close friends and just have it here. Have Belinda's Bakery cater the thing, and then dance all night with the woman you love. Make her happy, Rob."

Rob sighed and looked up at the ceiling before grabbing the ball off his desk. He began throwing it up in the air over and over, and Bailey watched him with a small smile on her face. A few moments later he caught it and looked at her. "Sometimes I can be a jerk, you know?"

Bailey grinned and stood up, walking over to her brother and hugging him. "You like the show, Rob. We all know that. But Wren can't do that. Forget about all your baseball buddies and showing off your gorgeous wife to them. It's not about that anyways. It's just about two people, who miraculously fell in love with each other, and want to start their lives together. Forget the show. Just think of Wren."

Rob nodded and patted her hand as he smiled up at her. "You are the best sister a guy could have, Bailey."

Bailey laughed and sat down again glancing at the door. "Taryn hears you say that, and your life won't be worth living."

Rob shrugged. "I tell her the same thing too. But I mean it when I say it to you."

Bailey laughed. "Well, I hate to say it, but I'm bored. You've got my boyfriend working like a mad man in your evil kitchen, and I have nothing to do."

Rob nodded his head and frowned. "Make the rounds with me for old time's sake and then have dinner with me. We'll make Kam and Wren take breaks, and they can come sit with us."

Bailey grinned and stood up. "Let's do it."

Bailey followed Rob around the restaurant, greeting the diners and asking how their meals went. It warmed her heart the way Rob introduced her proudly as his sister and made her feel like a queen. Taryn ran out and hugged her too, but had to deal with a waitress meltdown and left almost immediately. A half an hour later, she and Rob were seated in the back and Brogan was bringing them steaks and smothered baked potatoes.

"I'm so used to all of Wren's creative seafood dishes, that I forget how wonderful a steak and potato can be sometimes," she murmured, before sinking her teeth into her perfectly prepared steak.

Rob grinned and took a bite too. "It was my suggestion actually. I like the way we're always changing things up, but sometimes the basics are nice too. *Wow*, this is amazing. I'm going to give Wren a raise."

Bailey laughed and took a sip of water. "How many raises is that now? Ten? *Twenty?*"

Rob reddened and grinned. "Does it matter? Pretty soon she'll be part owner of The Iron Skillet."

Bailey smiled, happy her brother was so happy, and had found someone so perfect for him. "Is Wren going to keep working at this pace, after you guys are married?"

Rob shook his head. "For a little while. We've talked and Wren wants to semi-retire when we start our family. She'll always be the creative force behind our menu though. But Kam will be taking over as head chef at that point."

Bailey paused and looked at Rob. "*Really?* Kam hasn't been to culinary school."

Rob nodded his head readily and took a bite of the potatoes. "Wren's been teaching him everything she knows. Those two work in complete harmony with one another. Wren says it's like he can read her mind. Kam's a natural in the kitchen. By the time Wren leaves, Kam will be more than ready to be head chef. He'll be amazing."

Bailey grinned and raised her water glass to her brother. "Does he know?"

Rob shrugged. "I was waiting to tell him. Of course, I wanted to wait to make sure he doesn't break my little sister's heart first."

Bailey stared at Rob with a raised eyebrow before he laughed. "Well, it's true."

Bailey gave up and smiled. "You're a good brother, but your Italian genes are showing again."

Rob looked up, his smile turning up at least 50 watts, and she knew without turning around Wren, had appeared. Wren collapsed next to Rob and smiled tiredly. "I've got an hour left in me I think, before I dissolve on the floor in a puddle of exhaustion."

Rob frowned and handed her his water glass. "Honey, you're working too hard. You're on break right now. What do you feel like eating?"

Wren shrugged and motioned toward Rob's plate. "Can I have some of your potatoes? I'm not that hungry."

Rob pushed his plate toward Wren and watched as she consumed all of his potatoes and half of his steak. Bailey grinned and gave her half her potatoes too.

"I feel so much better," Wren said, wiping her mouth with a napkin and drinking all of Rob's water. "So, Bailey, we haven't had a chance to talk lately. How's everything going? Your bruise looks so much better today."

Rob frowned and studied his sister's forehead. Bailey grimaced and looked away. She'd used a ton of makeup to cover the purple bruise, and by Rob's eagle eye look he knew it.

"I'm fine, Wren. You should see the other guy," she said, and Rob cracked a smile, relaxing again.

Wren laughed and kicked her feet up on the empty chair

besides Bailey. "How are things with Kam? He sure looks happy these days. He's always singing and smiling and joking around with everyone."

Rob laughed at that. "Kam is *always* happy. When is he not singing and joking around."

Wren poked Rob in the side and frowned at him. "Not as much as he is now. And the songs have changed. Before, he'd sing whatever was playing on the radio, but now he's singing love songs. Today, he sang Mariah Carey's, *Vision of Love*. I'm not even kidding. Over and over. *And*, he hit the high note."

Rob's eyebrows went up and he turned to look at Bailey. Bailey laughed, turning red. "Well, it's true, Mariah Carey songs are a sure sign that someone's in love. What about you, Rob? What songs are you singing, now that Wren has stolen your heart?"

Rob laughed at having the tables turned on him and looked at Wren softly, as he took her hand in his. "I'm not the singer Kam is, but I do sing the Goo Goo Dolls, *Come to Me*. Every time I hear that song, I think of Wren."

Wren leaned over and kissed Rob. "I've just decided that will be the song that we dance to at our reception."

Rob grinned and touched Wren's cheek. "You'll be happy to know then, that you'll be dancing with me at our reception, right here at The Iron Skillet."

Wren's mouth dropped open as she stared at her fiancé. "Are you serious?" she whispered, raising her hands to her cheeks.

Rob laughed and nodded his head, glancing at Bailey. "My sister convinced me of the error of my ways. I just want to make you happy. No huge party with a bunch of drunken baseball players. Prepare for intimate and small."

Wren nodded her head and then surprised Rob and Bailey by wiping a tear off her cheek. "That's the sweetest thing. I know how much you wanted a big reception but you gave it up for me. I love you, Rob," she said, closing her eyes and lifting her chin.

Bailey watched her brother melt as his eyes softened. He

reached over and grabbed Wren's hand and glanced at Bailey. "I forgot I have to talk to Wren about something in my office. I'll be back in a few minutes," he said, and pulled Wren up and after him, as he walked out of the room.

Bailey grinned and took another bite of her steak. Wren was going to get the kiss of her life, if she wasn't mistaken.

"*Bailey?* I was hoping I'd find you here."

Bailey twisted around in her seat and looked up to see Dean Hogan standing beside her, looking impeccable in a dark suit and red tie. She swallowed her bite, and nodded her head. "*Dean . . .* why were you looking for me?"

Dean motioned for Rob's abandoned seat, and she nodded her assent. He sat down and moved Rob's plate out of the way, before leaning towards her. "You haven't answered any of my texts or voicemails. I'm worried about you, sweetheart."

Bailey blinked in surprise at the term of endearment. "Dean, there's no reason for you to be worried about me. We went out a few times. We're basically just acquaintances."

Dean frowned and shook his head. "That's not the way I see it. Bailey, I have feelings for you. I care about you. You have to know that. When that article came out, and I felt all of the pain you'd been holding inside, I was truly amazed by your strength. After reading about your struggle and seeing what an amazing and beautiful woman you've turned out to be, I just knew that you were the woman for me."

Bailey's mouth fell open as she stared in wonder at the man sitting across from her. "You've got to be kidding me," she whispered.

Dean smiled winningly and shook his head. "Not at all. You have to admit, you and I had three amazing dates together. We click, Bailey. We're so easy with one another. I've decided that I'd like to date you more seriously."

Bailey looked away from Dean's intent stare and felt uneasy. This was not good. "Dean, the last conversation we had at the bakery, you told me how much you wanted to date Wren, our head chef. You told me how you had plans to date all the women you could for a year, before picking the best one. I'm sorry, but that's when it ended for me."

Dean frowned and shook his head, not happy with what he was hearing. "Bailey, I can understand why you'd be disconcerted to know that I wasn't interested in making a commitment to you at that time, but that's all changed now. *I am* ready now. I've looked at all the variables and I've made my decision. There's no way I could find someone better than you. I know that now," he said, reaching across the table and taking her hand in his.

Bailey frowned and pulled on her hand. "Dean, *no* . . ."

"Who's the suit?"

Bailey's head whipped up to see Kam standing beside her, looking dark, dangerous and not happy. She pulled harder on her hand and Dean finally let her go.

"Kam, this is Dean Hogan. He's an acquaintance of mine," she said lamely.

Kam crossed his arms over his chest and glanced back and forth between Dean and Bailey. Dean, being oblivious to the dangerous undercurrents, smiled up at Kam and motioned toward Bailey.

"I'm doing my best to convince this beautiful woman, she belongs with me. We were made for each other."

Kam nodded his head as if he agreed. "Well, you do look good together, I'll give you that."

Dean laughed in delight. "That's what I think too. She's perfect for me. And I'd be the perfect choice for her. I've brought my resume for her to look over while she considers it. I'm completely ready to be a husband and provider. She'll never have to want for anything and she'll never find a better husband."

Bailey felt her stomach drop as she heard Dean go on and on, making things worse with every word he said.

Bailey stood up and grabbed Kam's hand. "Dean, I hate to

interrupt your speech, but I'd like to introduce you to my *boyfriend*, Kam Matafeo."

Dean's smile slowly faded as he looked from Kam to Bailey in confusion. "You can't be serious, Bailey. Does this man *work* here? You're dating a . . . *cook?*"

Bailey felt Kam stiffen next to her and she slipped her hand around his waist as she nodded her head. "Kam is a chef and I love him. And if you'll excuse us, it's time for him to take his break with me, and you're sitting in his spot."

Dean slowly stood up, still looking confused as he glanced at Kam again, shaking his head as if he couldn't believe it. "We'll talk about this late,r Bailey. In the meantime, I hope you'll still consider speaking to my group, about your experiences."

Bailey watched him walk away and then slowly lifted her face to look at Kam. Kam looked down at her, his eyes wary and his jaw hard.

"Why were you having dinner with Dean?" he asked, in a deceptively soft voice.

Bailey shook her head and gestured for Kam to take a seat. She motioned for Brogan to bring Kam something to eat before sitting down. Kam was sitting down now, but he looked very distant. She leaned forward, clasping her hands on the table. "I was not having dinner with Dean. Rob and I were eating, but he decided to take Wren back to his office for a kiss. That's his plate. *Not Dean's.* Dean showed up just now, and said he'd been trying to get in touch with me. He sat down and started telling me how he and I were perfect for each other, and then you showed up. I had no idea, Kam. *Honestly.*"

Kam let out a long sigh and looked away from her, across the dining room. He looked tired and unhappy, and Bailey wished she could erase the strain from his face.

"Remember when we were at your mom's house, and you told me that you were hesitant to date me, because we were so different?"

Bailey bit her lip and nodded silently.

Kam finally looked at her and his eyes looked impossibly sad. "Maybe you were right."

Bailey turned white as she stood up and grabbed Wren's vacated chair, so she could sit next to Kam. She grabbed his face in her hands and shook her head. "I was an idiot, Kam. We're not so different after all. *I love you.* All the things that I thought would pull us apart, are the things now that I love the most about you."

Kam's eyes softened slightly but his face remained hard and his body stiff. "I don't know, Bailey. Maybe Dean is right. Maybe you should think about our relationship before we take this any further."

Bailey let her hands fall from Kam's face as she shook her head. "What are you saying to me?" she whispered.

Kam must have realized how shocked she was, because he sat up and took her hands in his. "That man just sat there in front of me, and was honestly horrified at the thought of someone like you, being with a lowly cook. I have a feeling that most of your friends and coworkers will have the same reaction. You might want to take that into consideration."

Bailey swallowed, feeling nauseated. She let her eyes drop from Kam's before standing up and taking her seat across from him. She picked up the napkin in her hands and folded it in halves for a minute. "Does this sudden concern over what everybody else thinks about our relationship, have anything to do with the fact that your ex-girlfriend being back in town?" she asked quietly.

Kam massaged his temples and stood up. "No, Bailey, it doesn't. Look, I've got to get back to work. I'll call you," he said tersely, and walked away.

Bailey watched him go and felt her heart pound painfully in her chest. She stood up on shaky legs, just as Brogan walked up with Kam's dinner in his hands.

"Wait, is Kam coming back?" Brogan asked in confusion.

Bailey tried to smile and shook her head. "I'm afraid that

Kam has decided to take his dinner in the kitchen. Sorry, Brogan," she whispered, before walking quickly away and out of the restaurant.

She drove home, her hands stiff on the steering wheel as tears fell freely. *Kam Matafeo had just broken up with her.* She wiped her eyes and parked her car, sitting there for almost an hour, before finally walking through the rain to her apartment. She locked her door and then collapsed on her bed, not bothering to change out of her clothes, or even wash her face or brush her teeth. She ignored her ringing cell phone and finally fell into a fitful sleep. The banging on her front door woke her up at midnight, but she didn't bother getting up. She was positive that she didn't want to talk to whoever it was.

Chapter Twenty-Two

FRAGILE HEARTS

Kam walked into work Tuesday morning, feeling on edge and murderous. He growled at Pule and nodded at everyone else. Wren smiled brightly at him and then blinked in surprise, hurrying to his side and touching his arm.

"Kam, what's wrong?" she asked quietly.

Kam shrugged and grabbed an apron, tying it tightly around his waist. "Not much. Only Bailey won't answer her phone, her email or her door. She's completely blocked me out. Just like that. *Done*," he said bitterly, running his hand over his dark glossy hair.

Wren's mouth fell open and she shook her head in distress. "Kam, no! Bailey is head over heels in love with you. You're mistaken."

Kam put his hands on his waist and stared at Wren silently. Wren paled and then glanced over her shoulder at the prep cooks. "Kam and I have to make a run to the store. Start prepping for lunch and we'll be back soon," she ordered, and then grabbed Kam's hand and pulled him back out of the restaurant, and over to the van she used for getting the seafood.

Kam shrugged and got in the van, leaning his head back against the seat as Wren drove away from the restaurant. She came to a stop at the city park and turned off the van, turning in her seat to stare at him.

"Rob and I went to Puyallup, so we've been gone all weekend. Rob would have said something if Bailey had told him anything, and she tells him everything."

Kam raised an eyebrow. "No, she doesn't, Wren."

Wren made a huffing sound and twisted her hands in her lap. "Start at the beginning. You two were fine Saturday night. I saw you. She came in and kissed you and told you she loved you, like she always does. Her face literally lights up when she touches you."

Kam closed his eyes as Wren's words tore at his heart. "Yeah, well, when Brogan told me Bailey was eating dinner and wanted me to take my break with her, I hurried out and found her little suit and tie sitting with her, telling her how beautiful she was, and how perfect they were for each other."

Wren frowned and shook her head. "Rob and I were eating with Bailey. Dean wasn't there."

Kam sighed and shook his head. "You were in Rob's office kissing."

Wren blushed and looked away. "Oh, right."

Kam smiled a little and then continued. "I stood right there listening to it all. Bailey realized I was there and stood up and introduced me as her boyfriend and Dean couldn't believe it. He said, *you can't be serious, Bailey. Does this man work here? You're dating a . . . cook?*"

Wren frowned and reached over to touch his arm. "And what did Bailey say?"

Kam shrugged. "She stuck up for me, but it just reminded me of all the reasons she refused to go out with me for so long. It was because of everything Dean was saying. We are so different, Wren. I told her maybe she should think about it and then she asked me if this had anything to do with my ex-girlfriend being back in town. I blew her off and stormed off like an idiot, and that's the last I've heard from or seen her."

Wren frowned at him, her eyes snappy looking. *"You broke up with her."*

Kam looked up in surprise. *"No!* Of course I didn't. Why would you even say that?"

Wren shook her head impatiently. "That's what Bailey thinks, Kam. She stuck up for you, she stood by you, and then you threw it in her face. And then when she asked about Meredith, you blew her off and walked away from her. Kam, Bailey is so vulnerable when it comes to men. You probably just shattered her with the way you handled that. She looks so tough and yeah, she'll jump into a fight if she has to, but when it comes to feelings, especially love, she's so fragile."

Kam closed his eyes, his throat working as Wren continued to rake him over the coals. He finally held up his hand and shook his head. "I can't take it anymore. Wren, . . . stop. *Please.* Just tell me what I can do to fix this."

Wren bit her lip and put her hand on the steering wheel as she stared out at the park where moms and children were showing up with blankets, balls and picnics. "I don't know, Kam," she said gently. "Bailey is different than Taryn and Rob. She's softer than they are. She's breakable."

Kam nodded his head. "And you think I broke her?"

Wren shrugged. "I don't know. The last time you saw her was Saturday night? It's *Tuesday,* Kam. We haven't heard from Bailey, I know that, but we thought she was busy with you all weekend. Let's drive over to her apartment. I'm going to check on her."

Kam nodded quickly and Wren drove over to Bailey's apartment complex. She turned off the van and stared at Kam pensively for a moment. "You stay here. She might not open the door if you're with me."

Kam closed his eyes and shook his head. "Fine. Just see if she's okay."

Wren ran for Bailey's door and pounded hard, calling out her name over and over. Five long minutes later, Bailey cracked the door open. "*Wren?* What are you doing here?" she asked, in a normal sounding voice.

Wren smiled brightly and put her foot in the door. "I just haven't seen you since Saturday and wanted to see how you're doing. I'm getting my wedding dress fitted this afternoon and I was wondering if you'd come with me. You can try on your bridesmaid's dress again, just to make sure it's perfect."

Bailey opened the door a little wider and Wren slipped in, shutting the door behind her and walking into the apartment. She glanced around the dark room and noticed the blinds were drawn. She turned and looked at Bailey and gasped a little. Bailey looked pale, sick and thin. She had no makeup on, and her hair looked like a rat's nest.

"When's the last time you ate?" Wren demanded, rushing to the kitchen and flipping on the light. She grabbed some eggs and cheese out of the fridge, and a bowl out of the cupboard. She cracked a couple eggs and began whisking as she slipped some butter in the pan and turned the heat on.

Bailey shrugged and sat down on a stool, resting her head wearily in her hands as she stared at Wren. "I can't remember. I've been sleeping a lot."

Wren frowned. "My mom used to sleep a lot. That's a sign of depression, Bailey," she said quietly, as she poured the eggs into the sizzling butter.

Bailey shrugged and closed her eyes. "I wouldn't be surprised. Kam broke up with me. Don't tell Rob though. I don't want him to fire Kam."

Wren winced and looked for a spatula. "Does *Kam* know he broke up with you?"

Bailey blinked in surprise. "Of course, he does. He was there. He wants me to marry a guy in a suit. He thinks we're too different now because of stupid Dean," she said, her voice strengthening with a hint of anger.

Wren sighed. "Dean is an idiot. Why would Kam listen to him?"

Bailey laid her head on the counter. "I don't know, Wren. I think he just wanted an excuse to go back to Meredith. Why else would he walk away from me?"

Wren shook her head. "Bailey, I don't think Kam broke up with you. I understand that maybe it *felt* like he did. Maybe it even sounded like he did, but I don't think he did. I um, talked to him this morning, and he told me that he's been trying to call you all weekend."

Bailey licked her dry lips and sighed. "I don't care anymore. Isn't that interesting? I thought my heart would break into a million pieces Saturday night, but right now, I don't really care."

Wren flipped the omelet and grabbed the bag of shredded cheese as she glanced over at Bailey worriedly. "Bailey, you can't feel anything because you're dehydrated, hungry and not thinking right. You're going to eat this omelet, drink a few glasses of water and then take a shower. What would Rob and Taryn think if they were here right now?"

Bailey slowly raised her head and sat up, a worried frown on her face. "They would hate it and they'd throw a fit."

Wren nodded her head. "If you don't eat this whole omelet and drink everything I give you and do everything I say, I'm calling Rob and Taryn right now."

Bailey blanched and took the omelet from Wren and ate the whole thing obediently. She drank two glasses of water, took the Tylenol Wren handed her, and then took a shower. Wren glanced at the clock and winced at the time, but knew that Rob would rather have her there helping Bailey, than prepping for lunch.

When Bailey finally came out of the bedroom wearing fresh clothes, her hair wet and clean, Wren smiled in relief. Her eyes weren't so foggy looking anymore. She looked like Bailey, but now she looked heartbroken. She'd waken her up, that's for sure.

"Thanks, Wren. Thanks for checking on me. Please don't tell Rob and Taryn. I think I'm allowed to have a bad weekend after Saturday night. I'll be fine. I called into work sick today, but I'll be up and back to normal tomorrow."

Wren nodded in relief and glanced around the still dark apartment. "Will you call Kam? Will you please tell him you're okay? He's worried."

Bailey smiled faintly and shook her head. "No, but you can tell him I'm fine. Tell him that I don't blame him for wanting Meredith over me. She's cute and feisty and *normal*. I should have realized he wouldn't really want to be with someone like me. Someone who . . ." she stopped, looking away.

Wren frowned. "You mean, someone who was hurt?"

Bailey frowned and shook her head. "No, someone who's broken."

Wren groaned and walked over, pulling Bailey into her arms. She held her for a few moments, before pulling away and wiped a tear off of Bailey's cheek. "You're wrong about Kam. That's not how he sees you and that's not who you are. You told me that you were going to talk to Layla Bender. Can I call her for you? Can she come over and talk to you? Please?"

Bailey nodded, and sniffed. "That would probably be good."

Wren nodded and grabbed her cell phone out of her pocket. She texted Layla and put her phone away again. "I've got to get back to the restaurant. Will you be okay until Layla gets here?"

Bailey laughed a little. "Wren, I'm not suicidal. *Relax.* I just spent the weekend wallowing in a really bad break up. I'm fine. But please don't mention to my mom that I messed up another potential relationship. I don't think her bowling league can take it."

Wren grinned and touched Bailey's shiny blond hair. "Your secret is safe with me. Call me later, okay?"

Bailey nodded and walked her to the door. "Thanks, Wren. I love you."

Wren nodded and waved goodbye, not being able to say anything. She hurried back to the van and got in the driver's seat and turned the keys, backing out and driving quickly back to the restaurant.

"Well, you were gone for twenty minutes. You're not going to say anything? You're not going to tell me anything?"

Wren sighed and glanced at her friend. "You don't want to hear anything I could tell you."

Kam frowned darkly and looked out the window. "So, she does think I broke up with her? She thinks we're over?"

Wren nodded her head once. "She's convinced and nothing I said could change her mind. She thinks you were just looking for an excuse to break up with her, so you could be with a um . . . *normal* girl," she said quietly.

Kam was completely still for a moment before clenching his hands on his knees and making a growling sound in his throat, that had Wren looking at him in alarm.

"Is she okay?" he finally asked.

Wren pursed her lips, wondering what his definition of okay was. "I *think* so," she finally said. "Layla Bender is going to go over and talk to her this afternoon, but yeah, I think she'll be okay."

Kam massaged his chin. "Will she see me? Will she let me explain and make things right?"

Wren winced and looked away from him. "Remember when I told you Bailey was different from Rob and Taryn? Well, she's similar in some ways too. She can be really stubborn and she's got all the Downing pride. That, combined with her vulnerability and you have yourself a problem even bigger than anything Rob or Taryn could create. Her walls are going to be bulletproof now."

Kam stared gloomily out the window as Wren pulled up to the restaurant. She reached over and touched his arm. "There's still hope, Kam."

Kam glanced at her and shook his head. "Really, what hope do I have?"

Wren smiled. "She's completely in love with you. Where there's love, there's hope."

Kam got out of the van and trudged back inside without

answering her. He went to work, ignoring everyone and every-thing, except what was in front of him. He got through the day, but as soon as he was done, he left and drove down to the beach. He'd just messed everything up. He'd had everything. He'd had the woman he loved and he messed up, because his pride had been hurt. Being trashed in front of Bailey by Dean, had made him furious and he'd taken it out on Bailey. He could be honest about it. That's exactly what he'd done and he'd hurt her horribly because of it.

He stared up at the stars and thought about what Wren had said about hope. If Bailey still loved him, he was going to get her back. He sighed tiredly and stood up, walking back to his car. Tomorrow was a new day and Bailey didn't know it, but she was going to be his again. He swore right then that he'd never let anyone or anything tear them apart again.

Chapter Twenty-Three

DRAMA QUEEN

Bailey waved goodbye to Layla and smiled a little. She'd come over Tuesday afternoon and again on Wednesday morning. She had to get to work soon, but now, she felt like she could. Layla had walked her through everything and had very calmly and very firmly told her she was being immature and silly. Bailey grinned and laughed a little at herself. Layla was a tough woman, but she saw through to the core of things and after talking to Layla, she had to agree with her.

She grabbed her laptop and her keys and headed to her car. Time to get back to life, and time to grow up a little. She'd let a little fight with Kam explode into something huge and dark and ugly and she'd totally overreacted. She bit her lip as she blushed a little at how silly she'd been. *Poor, Wren,* she must have been horrified when she'd seen her. But, bless her heart, she hadn't said a word to Rob or Taryn, because nobody had busted down her door. On the other hand, she must have said *something* to Kam, because his texts and calls had stopped immediately.

She frowned and wondered what Wren had told him. She pulled into the News Tribune's parking lot and showed her pass to the security guard. She waved at everyone as she made her way to her cubicle, but stopped when she saw a large vase of deep red roses sitting on her desk.

What in the world?

She snatched the card out of the vase and ripped open the envelope. If these were from Dean, they were going in the garbage can.

Baby, I love you. Please forgive me for losing my temper and taking it out on you. Let's have dinner together tonight in Tacoma. There's a new Japanese restaurant I'd like to take you to. Text me to let me know where you want me to pick you up. Love you, Kam

Bailey closed her eyes and held the card to her lips. *Kam.* Should she? Or should she take some time to herself, to make sure she was stable enough and strong enough to be in a relationship? She frowned and sent a text to Layla.

Am I too insane to be in a relationship right now? Should I take some time off to grow up?

Bailey stared at her phone and jumped when it vibrated almost immediately.

Stop being such a chicken. Love is always going to be scary. Get over it.

Bailey laughed a little and then kissed the card, before putting it back on the stick in her flowers.

She spent the rest of the day catching up on work and writing a small article on a local election coming up, before she took a few minutes and finally texted Kam.

I'm working today, but I can meet you at the restaurant at six.

A few seconds later she got a reply.

K Love you Baby

Bailey grinned and went back to work, happier than she'd been in days. Maybe it was possible for her to love Kam? After work, she hurried home to take a quick shower and fix her hair and makeup. She changed into a simple white skirt, heels and a turquoise silk shirt, before driving over to the restaurant. She parked her car in the back, right next to Kam's suburban and then walked slowly to the back door. She hadn't been back to

The Iron Skillet since that horrid Saturday night Kam had
dumped her. She touched the door knob and took a deep breath
before slowly pushing it open. She walked in and let her eyes
adjust, and saw Pule looking at her with wide eyes.

She smiled and waved and then walked further into the
kitchen. And stopped dead in her tracks.

Meredith.

Meredith plastered to Kam.

Again.

Kam was patting Meredith's back soothingly as he talked
quickly and softly. She watched as Meredith shook her head
vigorously back and forth.

"But I heard you two broke up. I heard she dumped you for
some rich guy."

Kam frowned and disengaged one of Meredith's hands from
his shirt. "Feke is gossiping again, huh? Well, he misheard me.
And we're *not* broken up. As a matter of fact, we're going out to
dinner tonight, so you really need to leave before she gets here."

Meredith stared miserably up at Kam and shook her head.
"Kam, I don't get it," she whispered. "Before I left, we were so
great together. We had so much fun, and I liked you so much.
We could have that again. I heard about your girlfriend. I read
those articles she wrote. Tawni showed them to me. She's gotta
be messed up from all of that crap that happened to her. Do you
really want to have to deal with all of her hang ups? I know she's
pretty and everything, but she can't be all right after that, Kam."

Kam glared at Meredith and pushed her away from him.
"You don't know anything about her, Meredith. She's strong and
beautiful and good, and she's so full of love she doesn't even
know how to control it sometimes."

Bailey blinked in surprise and licked her lips. He might have
a point. She looked back up at Meredith and saw that dangerous
light go on in her eyes again.

"You're just saying that to hurt me. You're getting back at me
because I left you."

Kam sighed and ran his hands through his long dark hair. "Meredith just stop. If you had loved me, *really loved me*, you wouldn't have left me in the first place."

Meredith looked away and wiped her eyes. "It was after I left, that I realized how much I love you, Kam. Can't we just start over?"

Kam didn't say anything for a long time. "Meredith, right now, I don't know how things are going to play out with Bailey."

Bailey blinked slowly at that. He was going to keep Meredith on the side, until he lost interest in her and then he'd go back to Meredith. She slowly turned on her heels and headed back for the door.

Pule cleared his throat loudly and Kam glanced over at him. Bailey felt the exact moment when Kam's eyes touched on her, because she felt the familiar spark of electricity. She heard him yell her name, just as she disappeared through the backdoor. She glanced at her car but ignored it and sprinted around the building. She gasped and then wrenched open the front door of The Iron Skillet and rushed through. She bypassed Rob's office and headed to Taryn's office, further down the hallway. Behind her, she could hear Kam yelling her name and put on a burst of speed. She ran into Taryn's office and shut the door quietly, locking it behind her. She hurried to Taryn's desk and glanced at her calendar. *Perfect.* She was having a business dinner with suppliers tonight.

She heard someone rattle the doorknob and call her name before footsteps hurried away. She let out a sigh of relief and sat down in Taryn's cushy chair. She'd wait until Kam gave up looking for her, and then sneak out. As all of the adrenaline from her escape left her, she felt suddenly hollow and cold.

Kam couldn't really love her if he was willing to keep Meredith as a backup. She leaned her head back and commanded herself not to cry. She'd done enough of that over the weekend. She stared down at her three inch heels that brought her to within a few inches of Kam's height and wished she'd worn jeans and her tennis shoes instead. Not the best getaway outfit.

She waited an hour and then slowly opened the door, peeking out into the dim hallway. Totally clear. She slipped out of the office, smoothed her hair down and then walked calmly down the hallway, wincing at the loud clicking sound her heels made on the hard tile. She paused and slipped her feet out of the heels and carried them by their straps as she reached the corner. She peeked around the wall and saw Brittany flirting with a waiter. It was one of their slow nights. If it had been busy, she could have slipped out without anyone even noticing. She took a deep breath and let it out. She could do this. She straightened her shoulders and then walked confidently toward the front door, smiling brightly at Brittany.

"Hey, Brittany, tell Taryn I came by to see her but that I'll catch up with her later," she said breezily, speeding up as she reached for the door.

"Hi, Bailey. *Oh, wait.* Kam said if I saw you, to tell him. He said he really wants to talk to you and that it's extremely urgent," Brittany said, frowning and glancing over her shoulder in the direction of the kitchen.

Bailey smiled and laughed a little. "Oh, don't worry about it, Brittany. I'll talk to Kam later. I've actually got a date so I need to hurry. Bye," she lied, and wrenched open the door.

Freedom.

She looked both ways and then remembered she had to get her car parked in back. Right next to Kam's. Maybe he gave up and left? She hurried around the corner and peeked around the corner. Not a soul in sight. Easy. She sprinted over the hard pavement in her bare feet, wincing and moaning at the pain. She opened her car door and jumped in, sighing in relief. She glanced in her mirrors to make sure no one was running after her and then quickly put her car in reverse and drove out of the parking lot. So easy.

She smiled triumphantly to herself and then turned toward

home. She had been expecting Japanese food and now she was starving. She'd just go through a drive through and grab a few tacos instead. She drove up to the window and leaned out.

"I'll have three tacos and a large drink please," she said, with a smile.

"I'll have the steak and bean burrito, a few tacos and a large drink too."

Bailey screamed and turned around to see Kam sitting in her backseat. Her mouth fell open as he grinned at her.

"So that's six tacos, two large drinks and a steak and bean burrito?"

Bailey turned back to the drive through window and nodded dumbly, taking out her wallet and handing him her credit card. She sat silently as she waited for him to give her the food and her card back. In the meantime, Kam got out and walked around to the front, getting in and sitting next to her.

She took the bag of food and handed the drinks to Kam before driving away. "Where do you want me to drop you off?" she asked politely.

Kam smiled genially and shrugged. "I'm with you tonight. We had a date, remember? I was planning on Japanese food, but I like tacos too."

Bailey's mouth tightened and she drove to Kam's house. When she stopped the car, she handed him the bag of tacos and gestured to the door. "Enjoy your dinner. *Alone.*"

Kam frowned and shook his head. "I'm not leaving until we settle this, Bailey. Now knock it off, and let's go somewhere we can talk in private. You don't want to discuss our love life in front of my mom and dad, and all of my brothers and sisters."

Bailey rolled her eyes and drove away. She grinned and headed to the local cemetery. He wanted to talk about love? *Fine.* She hoped he was scared of ghosts.

Kam sighed loudly as she pulled into the cemetery. "*Really, Bailey?*"

Bailey turned off the car and smiled. "Romance is dead to

me. Talk away," she said, and grabbed the bag of tacos, taking out one and opening a hot sauce packet. She took a big bite as Kam sat and stared at her. She gestured with her hands for him to get on with it.

"This is where you tell me that I didn't hear you tell your ex-girlfriend, to stick around, because things probably wouldn't work out with me anyways."

Kam's face tightened and she smiled brightly at him. "Hand me my drink will you? This inferno hot sauce is actually almost hot."

Kam handed her the drink and sat back staring at her. "Why is it that you misinterpret everything I say? On Saturday night, you thought I broke up with you."

Bailey nodded and took another bite. "*You did*. We're too different you said. And then you walked away."

Kam's eyes darkened and he folded his arms across his chest. "I was hurt, Bailey. My heart and my pride were hurt. I'd just stood there and listened to your little suit tell me I wasn't good enough for you. Was I supposed to be happy about that?" he asked quietly.

Bailey paused and licked her lips. "And why would you care what he thought about us anyways?"

Kam shrugged. "I'm human. No one likes to be degraded or put down. I was judged and found wanting. I didn't take it well."

Bailey shrugged. "Whatever. Life goes on," she said flippantly, with a smile. "So, *Meredith*, now she's just so cute. So spunky. And *so* in love with you too. And like she so kindly pointed out, completely normal and not messed up at *all*. You know, like me. She's a real catch, Kam. You should grab her while you can. Oh, that's right. *You just did*," she said, her eyes cold and furious.

Kam groaned and ran his hands through his hair, making his pony tail come loose. "She didn't know you were standing there. She wouldn't have said that, if she'd known you were there," he said patiently.

Bailey smiled coldly at him. "Isn't that sweet how you jump to defend her? It's actually kind of touching. But, so what? It's what she thinks. It's what you think. Right, Kam?"

Kam shook his head silently. "I'm really messing this up. *Again*. Please, just listen to me, Bailey. When I said, I don't know right now, that I don't know how things are going to play out with you, I just meant that I didn't know what your feelings were for me anymore. After Saturday night, I didn't know if you even wanted to be with me anymore."

Bailey rolled up her Taco wrapper into a tight ball and threw it in the paper bag. "Here's what I think. You said, *I don't know, Meredith*, because you were telling her that there was hope for you and her to get back together."

Kam frowned darkly and looked away from her. "I can see how you would think that, but no, Bailey, I don't want to get back together with Meredith. Even if you break up with me right now and you leave me and you never talk to me again, I won't go back to Meredith."

Bailey picked up her drink and touched the condensation on the side. "Why, Kam? Why not? You two are perfect for each other," she said quietly.

Kam nodded his head. "Maybe in some ways, but she's not the woman for me. When she broke up with me and left me, so she could move to California, I was hurt and sad but I wasn't broken hearted. If I had been, I would have followed her to California. I would have done everything in my power to win her back. I didn't. Because in my heart, I didn't really want to."

Bailey licked her lips and looked out the window. "Yeah, well, when you broke up with me Saturday night, you called a few times, but you seemed fine letting me go."

Kam snorted and stared at her with hot gleaming eyes. "*Fine?* You don't know anything about it. I was a mess. I yelled at everybody at work on Tuesday. I've been fighting with everyone. I sat in the car while Wren checked on you, because I was worried sick about you. And just now, when you ran away from me, I waited in your cramped, tiny car for an hour, because I knew that would be the only way to catch you. Bailey, you're a lot of work, sweetheart, but you're worth it, because I love you. I love you with all of my heart, body and soul. I love you," he said, moving toward her.

He reached over and took her hand in his. "I love you," he whispered, before reaching out and touching her cheek, turning her face toward his. "I love you," he said, his voice hoarse with emotion.

Bailey finally looked at him and shuddered as he leaned over and kissed her gently on the lips. "I love you," he said again, his voice stronger. He kissed her again and took her drink out of her hands, and put it on the dash as he pulled her over onto his lap. "I love you," he said, his voice firm with conviction. Bailey felt his arms wrap around her and she clenched her eyes shut.

Could she believe him? Could she really truly believe that Kam would love her above every other woman? Could she believe that he really would love her, cracks and damage and all?

"I love you, Bailey."

Bailey let out a breath as she felt him nuzzle her neck and felt herself weakening.

"And do you want to know what's really amazing? You love me too."

Bailey sniffed and fought back the tears that had been hiding behind her eyes all along.

"You love me so much, it terrifies you, because loving me gives me the ability to hurt you. Bailey, I never want to hurt you and I have and I'm so sorry. I'm sorry I let my anger and pride hurt you. I'm sorry Meredith hurt you, and that what I said hurt you. Will you forgive me?"

Bailey shook her head and pulled back from Kam. "I can't forget what you said, Kam. I don't care what you say now, I heard you tell Meredith that she could wait around for you, because we might not happen. Which by the way, is kind of a jerk move in regards to Meredith. No woman should have to wait around for a man to lose interest in another woman. Really lame, Kam," she said, with her nose in the air.

Kam ran his hands soothingly over her back and laughed a little. "Baby, I didn't know what to say to Meredith. I was honestly just trying to get her to leave. I probably would have told her I'd marry her next week, just to get her to take off. The last time you two were in the same room, some very innocent potatoes were injured. I couldn't risk another fight. I didn't think Meredith would survive another round with you."

Bailey turned away to hide her smile. "Stop trying to charm me, Kam."

Kam made a grunting noise. "Bailey, it's the truth. She had been there fifteen minutes by the time you must have arrived. I looked at the clock and realized you were going to be there any minute and panicked. Before I heard Pule clear his throat, I was getting ready to tell her that I'd meet her for lunch tomorrow, so we could talk it out."

Bailey whipped her head around and glared at him, her eyes bright and hot. "Oh, you were," she hissed, trying to climb off his lap.

Kam laughed and held on. "Just to get her out of there! Listen to me, Bailey, it was all out of self-preservation."

Bailey pushed on his shoulder but he didn't budge. "And would you have? Would you have met her for lunch?"

Kam nodded his head. "Of course, I would have brought Tate with me, but all in the hopes of convincing her to stop. Bailey, I *don't* love Meredith. I mean, I did. I did love her. But now that I've been with you, I know now that I was never *in* love with her. Because I know what that feels like now."

Bailey stopped struggling and turned and looked at Kam, her eyes, wide and vulnerable and soft. "Kam, I am begging you not to lie to me. I . . . I can't *handle* it," she whispered. "If you love me, you can't push me away. If you love me, I can't be wondering if you want to be with some ex-girlfriend of yours. I'm not as tough as you think I am. Doubts kill me. They hurt me and I bleed inside. I bleed a lot and I'm tired of pain. So, for my sake, tell me once and for all if you love me. All the way, no matter what, forever. Because if you don't, and you have doubts, or a part of you really does miss Meredith, I'm begging you to walk away from me right now, while I have a chance to get over you," she whispered.

Kam stared at her silently for a moment, his eyes dark and intense as he pulled her closer. He reached up and pulled her hair over her shoulder and then touched her cheek. "What have I been asking you practically from the first moment I met you?" he asked softy.

Bailey frowned and looked down at his chest. She touched his stone necklace and bit her lip. "You asked me to have faith in love."

Kam nodded once and touched her collar bone lightly following it to her shoulder. "I've been telling you non-stop that I love you, Bailey, but none of that matters if you won't have faith in me."

Bailey closed her eyes and leaned her forehead against his shoulder as she struggled with her inner demons. "It's so hard for me to trust people."

Kam kissed her cheek and followed the bones of her spine down her back over her silk shirt. "But not impossible. Bailey, hear my heart when I tell you that I will always love you. I will always be true to you. I'll *never* betray you."

Bailey lifted her head and stared into Kam's dark and hot eyes. She nodded her head slowly once and let out her breath. "I believe you," she whispered, and watched curiously as his eyes lit up, before he pulled her close for a hug that lasted for what seemed like forever.

She pulled away and leaned in to kiss him, but he shook his head. "No way am I going to sit in a car and kiss you in a cemetery."

She laughed and scooted back, sitting in her seat. She started the car and drove them out of the cemetery.

"Where to?"

Kam grinned. "I'm taking you to a Japanese restaurant in Tacoma. Head for the freeway."

Bailey frowned and looked at the bag full of tacos and one very large steak burrito. "But I just bought you dinner. I just ate a taco!"

Kam laughed. "Well, now you get to eat some sushi too. And let that be a lesson to you. When a man asks you out, don't try and hijack the date with fast food. It's not nice."

Bailey laughed and looked over at Kam smiling back at her. They spent the rest of the night talking and eating and becoming comfortable with each other again. When she drove him back to his car in the parking lot of The Iron Skillet, he leaned down and kissed her through the window. Bailey reached through the window and touched his dark silky hair and sighed happily. Kam Matafeo somehow knew how to tell her he loved her through a simple kiss. She could feel his love for her wrap around her more tightly than his arms.

They slowly pulled away from each other and smiled. "Love you, Baby," he said softly.

"I love you, Kam," she said back, and then drove away.

She went to sleep that night feeling something hot and burning inside of her heart. She hadn't felt it in a long time. It was faith.

Chapter Twenty-Four

THE WEDDING

One month later

Bailey twirled around in her silver bridesmaid's dress that flew out around her.

"You look just like a little girl, twirling around for the fun of it."

Bailey laughed and reached out for Kam's hand. "That's probably because I'm twirling around for the fun of it. Don't you ever do anything just for the fun of it?"

Kam laughed. "Every day. Kissing you is the most fun I have, and I do it as much as possible."

Bailey grinned and lifted her face away before he could swoop in and prove his point. "You can't mess up my makeup. Wren would kill me. We have pictures right after the ceremony."

Kam glared at her but sighed and held out his arm for her. She smiled and walked with him into the church. He escorted her past all of the guests and she smiled regally as Kam tried not fidget with the tux that was too tight around the shoulders and too big around his hips.

"You look great. Stop pulling on it," she said, out of the corner of her mouth.

Kam frowned and whispered back. "I just felt two seams pop."

Bailey snorted and tried to hold in a giggle as her mom came into view. She winked at her mom and went to stand next to Taryn, who was already in place. Jane and Kit and Layla joined her next, followed by Wren's little sister Poppy. Bailey smiled at Kam who was staring at her still, and then looked at Rob who looked nervous but happy too. Tate was there, along with Michael and Hunter and Wren's older brother Vick who was in a wheelchair. The music started and she turned to see Wren walking toward them on the arm of her father. She heard a little sound of surprise come from her brother and glanced quickly at him. Everyone was looking at the bride, but if they were looking at Rob, they would have seen his heart in his eyes and they would have witnessed him wiping his eyes as Wren smiled at him.

Bailey sniffed back tears and watched as her brother promised God he'd love Wren. She knew he would too. Rob would spend his whole life making sure Wren knew she was loved. As the vows were spoken she looked at Kam and wondered if she'd ever have the chance to promise God to love Kam. Kam was ignoring Rob and Wren and staring right back at her. She smiled at him, her eyes telling him how she felt. Kam closed his eyes for a second before smiling at her. And then he mouthed the words that she'd never get tired of hearing.

I love you.

Bailey beamed at Kam. She mouthed the words back to him, hoping no one would see. Kam's eyes burned bright with happiness. And then he mouthed more words at her.

Will you marry me?

Bailey blinked in surprise and frowned, looking away. No way had she just read that right. She looked back at Kam, her eyes questioning. Kam nodded his head slightly, and did it again.

Will you marry me?

Bailey bit her lip as her face turned bright red. She glanced around the wedding party but all eyes were on Rob and Wren. She glanced back at Kam and now he looked impatient. His eyes turning intense the way they did sometimes.

Will you marry me?

Bailey bit her lip and knew that if there was one man she could have faith in, it was Kam Matafeo. She grinned and nodded her head once before mouthing one word.

Yes

First Chapter in Book 6 of the Fircrest Series:

Tough Love

Chapter Twenty-Five

THE PROBLEM WITH TARYN

Anne Downing smiled as she surveyed her crowded dining room table, and had to admit that she was thrilled that her children had been obedient and had done what they'd been told to do. *Get serious about love.* Her heart softened as her eyes rested on her son, Rob. He'd found love, *finally*, with a pretty little chef who could wrap him around her finger faster than she could sear a pan of scallops. They'd been married now for a few months and she could hardly wait until they gave her a grandchild to love.

She took a bite of her Caesar salad as she watched Wren lean over and whisper something in her son's ear, making him grin before leaning over and kissing her. Wren was a quiet little thing, but she had steel in her spine. She had to, to put up with Rob, that's for sure. They balanced each other out and in a strange way were perfect for each other. She'd had her heart set on having one of the Kendall sisters for a daughter-in-law, but in the end, God knew better.

Anne sighed happily and glanced at her youngest, Bailey and the man she'd chosen, Kam Matafeo. They were engaged to be married in a month and she was going crazy trying to keep up with all of the wedding details. Rob's wedding had been so easy, she'd been spoiled. Rob and Wren had the reception at The Iron

Skillet and had Belinda's Bakery cater the whole thing. All she'd had to do was pick out a dress and show up. Bailey was driving her nuts with samples of napkins, place settings and appetizers. It seemed like every day she was being dragged to dress fittings or cake tastings. Okay, so maybe she was in heaven, but it *was* a lot to keep up with.

It was all worth it, because her baby had finally allowed herself to fall in love. She shook her head as Kam fed Bailey from off his plate, as if she didn't have the exact same food on her own. That was Kam though. Always looking out for Bailey and so protective. Kam swooped down and kissed Bailey quickly, making her laugh and Anne knew Bailey had made the right choice. Kam would never be comfortable in a suit or climb the corporate ladder, but he was very successful at making her daughter happy, and in her book, that was the best success there was.

Anne picked up her water glass as her eyes drifted to her daughter, Taryn. Her middle child. Her trial. *The disobedient one.* Anne's happy smile faded as she watched Taryn eat quickly and systematically, as if she couldn't wait to be done with dinner so she could leave, as if a family dinner was something you should want to escape from.

Anne frowned as she watched Taryn glance at her watch, as if she had somewhere else to be. Taryn looked up quickly and laughed at something Rob said, and Anne felt a tightening in her heart. Of all her children, Taryn was the most like her, which is why they butted heads so often and so well. She was stubborn, smart *and knew it*, beautiful in a dramatic way, that intimidated people, but she also had a heart so big, she did everything she could to protect it. Even to the point of pushing the chance of love away, just so she wouldn't get hurt.

Anne took a bite of her salmon and sighed, wishing Taryn was more open to love. Rob had been easy. He'd actually wanted to get married and settle down. Bailey had been a surprise, falling in love quickly and passionately. But Taryn was fighting her every step of the way. The last man she'd tried to set Taryn up with, had been one of Rob's friends from Seattle, a successful accountant who Rob swore was one of the good guys. Taryn had put him off so many times, he'd lost interest and was now in a committed relationship with one of his CPA's.

For a while there, Anne had wondered if Taryn had feelings for Brogan Moore, but every time she brought it up, Taryn shook her head and changed the subject. When she'd asked Rob about Brogan, he had grimaced and told her to let it go. He'd said Taryn was determined to choose with her head and not her heart. Well, from where she was sitting, that wasn't going so well.

Anne watched silently as Taryn smiled at Rob ,as he put his arm around Wren's shoulder and smoothed her hair away from her face, in an intimate way, that had Taryn's eyes going sad and soft. Taryn then glanced across the table at Bailey and Kam who were so busy staring at each other, no one else mattered. Anne's heart hurt as Taryn sighed and closed her eyes as if she was in pain.

Yes, it was time that Taryn fell in love. *Long* past time.

"I can't wait for your engagement party next Friday, Bailey. I haven't had roasted pig since Jane's wedding," Anne said, glancing at Taryn quickly as she put her napkin over her plate, signaling she had maybe five minutes to make her point, if that.

Taryn glanced at her sister smiled. "Do you need my help with anything, Bailey?"

Bailey sighed happily as she leaned onto Kam's shoulder. "Just for you to show up with a hot date, that's all."

Anne grinned and winked at Bailey. Bailey winked back at her mom, as Taryn closed her eyes and groaned loudly.

"I don't *have* a date, I don't *want* a date and for the last time, I'm *not* bringing a date, so let's just drop it, okay?"

Rob frowned and reached over, touching Taryn's shoulder. "It's no big deal, Taryn. You can bring a friend. You don't have to be involved with someone, you know."

Bailey frowned and glanced at Kam. "Taryn, I thought you
and . . ."

Taryn whipped her head around and glared at Bailey, as she
shook her head quickly back and forth. "I'll come up with a date.
Let's just drop the subject, *okay?* Now, Jane told me that Kam is
going to have a bachelor party. Are you really going to allow that,
Bailey?"

Anne's eyebrows snapped up as Bailey turned on Kam and all
attention was now on him as he laughed and held up his hands,
trying to deny everything, as Bailey crossed her arms over her
chest and glared at him. Anne laughed and glanced back at
Taryn, and noticed she looked relieved. *What a little stinker.* She'd
thrown Kam under the bus, to get out of having to talk about
getting a date for the party.

Taryn stood up and walked around the table, leaning down to
kiss her on the cheek. "Gotta run, Mom. Dinner was great. Love
ya," she said, and then breezed out of the room without a back-
ward glance.

Anne frowned after her daughter and waited until the front
door shut before she held up a hand to get everyone's attention.

"*What* is going on with Taryn?" she demanded, staring down
everyone at the table.

Rob cleared his throat and looked up at the ceiling, not
saying anything. Wren bit her lip and looked at her plate. Kam
put a big bite of food in his mouth, so he wouldn't have to say
anything and Bailey's eyes went wide and innocent, as if she had
no idea what she was talking about. Anne narrowed her eyes at
the table before her eyes rested on Wren. *Bingo.*

"*Wren?* You know everything that happens in that restaurant.
Is there something going on with Taryn? You know I only want
my children to be happy. You have to know that Taryn's happiness is all that matters to me," she said plaintively.

Wren swallowed and looked at Rob, but he was studying his
cuticles, as if they were the most interesting thing in the world.
"Um, *well*, I think Taryn is doing just fine, Anne. She's under a

lot of pressure at work, of course, so she doesn't have a lot of time to socialize."

Anne frowned and tapped her fingers on the table. "Neither do you, but you fell in love and got married. It's hard, but not impossible. Is she interested in anyone?"

Kam winced as Wren's face reddened and jumped in for the rescue. "Anne, Taryn is trying to figure things out. I don't think we should expect her to come up with a date for the party."

Anne pursed her lips and sat forward. "Well, *I do* expect it, and if she won't, then I will. Robert, you are going to get your sister a date. A surprise date. If she won't do what she's supposed to do, then we'll just go over her head. Who do you know who is good-looking, nice, fun and successful?"

Rob groaned and tilted his head back. "Mom, if Taryn knew what you're planning, she'd throw a temper tantrum. Do we have to do this?"

Anne nodded her head quickly. "As if you have to ask. *Yes,* we're doing this. *You're* doing this. You have to know at least one man who fits those criteria."

Rob shrugged and looked away. "Mom, you know I've tried setting her up with friends of mine. She goes, she sneers, she sighs, she pouts and then she's done. You'll have better luck with Kam," he said, pointing at his future brother-in-law.

Kam blinked in surprise and then narrowed his eyes at Rob. Rob grinned evilly and picked up his fork, eating with gusto, now that he was off the chopping block.

Anne pursed her lips and considered Kam. "Do you know anyone older, successful, smart and worthy of my daughter?"

Kam sighed and glanced at Bailey, who was wincing noticeably. "Anne, I make it a point not to hang out with uptight guys in suits. I barely make an exception for Rob as it is. Most of my friends are blue collar guys, but they have good hearts and they're hard workers. None of my friends would be Taryn's type, I'm afraid."

Anne frowned and pushed her plate away. "Well, what are we going to do? *Huh?* She's the pickiest woman in the world."

Bailey pushed her long, blond hair over her shoulder and leaned forward. "Mom, can't we just let Taryn figure this out on her own?"

Anne shook her head and laughed as she gestured to the table. "I have one son happily married, and you're next. Why in the world would I want to leave this up to Taryn? I love my kids, but you're all helpless when it comes to love, and don't you dare deny it. Now, we're not leaving this table, until we come up with a man for your sister to take to the party. A man that she could fall in love with," she clarified.

Wren licked her lips and cleared her voice. "What about Garrett, Rob? You know, your buddy? He's a landscaper, right? You and Michael hung out with him just last week."

Rob's eyes went big as he stared at Wren. "You want me to set *Taryn* up with *Garrett?*"

Wren smiled and nodded her head. "Well, he's flat out gorgeous, he's a veteran and he runs that landscaping business. *And*, he's really hot."

Rob frowned and sat up, his eyes narrowing. "You said that already. Why are you noticing how good looking he is?" he asked, in a calm voice, as his eyes turned dark.

Wren lifted her eyebrows and shrugged as she began to grin. "It was an accident. What do you think, Anne?"

Anne clapped her hands and grinned. "He'll do perfectly. And if he's as good looking as you say he is, Wren, then Taryn will thank us later."

Rob stood up and grabbed Wren's hand in his. "Sorry, but I just remembered that Wren and I have someplace to be right now," he said, and pulled his giggling wife out of the room.

Anne rolled her eyes. "Rob is so silly."

Kam laughed and held Bailey's hand. "He's a jealous man, Anne. Very passionate. I still remember the time he tackled me, because he thought Wren and I were dating."

Bailey sniffed and covered her plate with her napkin. "I felt like tackling you myself."

Kam grinned and kissed the back of her hand. "That's right, Rob's not the only one with jealousy issues."

Bailey glared at Kam. "Well, I for one can't wait to meet Garrett. I should probably meet him first, just to make sure he's really as cute as Wren says he is."

Kam raised an eyebrow. "Oh, really?"

Bailey raised an eyebrow back. "*Really.*"

Kam stood up and grabbed Bailey's hand in his. "Anne, dinner was amazing. Thanks so much for having us over, but we have to leave now."

Anne watched as Kam picked up Bailey, who was laughing now, and carried her out of the room. She listened to the front door shut and sat back in her chair. Had she ever been so silly and passionate and in love? She grinned and stood up, walking over to stare at the old and faded wedding portrait, of her and her husband, Pat. She touched the picture and sighed, missing her husband. *She had been exactly like that.*

She turned away and stared out the window at the gray clouds and nodded her head. Taryn would know what it felt like to fall in love. She was determined.

ACKNOWLEDGMENTS

As always, thanks to Jessica Guymon and Christina Tarbet.

Biography

I live in the Rocky Mountains with my husband and children and love my home when it's not snowing. I'm the author of 37 books so far. I also write YA Paranormal Romance under my pen name, Katie Lee O'Guinn. I enjoy the outdoors, reading and being with my family. To find out the latest on my books, check out my blog. You can purchase all of my books at Amazon.com. I'm also a huge supporter of Operation Underground Railroad. Check out their website to learn more.

BOOKS BY SHANNON GUYMON

Fircrest Series

You Belong With - Me Book 1

I Belong With You - Book 2

My Sweetheart - Book 3

Come To Me - Book 4

Be Mine - Book 5

Tough Love - Book 6

Falling for Rayne - Book 7

Dreaming of Ivy - Book 8

A Passion for Cleo - Book 9

My One and Only - Book 10

Free Fallin' - Book 11

At Last - Book 12

Accidentally in Love - Book 13

The Belfast Series

Love and Karma - Book 1

BOOKS BY KATIE LEE O'GUINN (PEN NAME) - CLEAN YA PARANORMAL ROMANCE

The Lost Witch Trilogy

Freak of Nature

Blood Rush

Fate Changer

Taming the Wolf Series

Werewolf Dreams

Werewolf Rage

Werewolf Revenge

Werewolf Betrayal

Chasing the Wolf Series

Hunted

Taken

Lost

Box Sets

The Lost Witch Series

Taming the Wolf Series